RETURN TO AKADA

Rich widow Rita Perrivale returns to the coast of West Africa on a new expedition to the legendary lost city of Akada and its treasures. She only survived the first, disastrous expedition due to the help of Anjani, a white man, raised in the jungle by a native tribe. But Rita, hoping to be reunited with Anjani, hasn't reckoned with the treacherous Tocoto, Anjani's twin brother — and his rival for the supremacy of the Dark Continent . . .

JOHN RUSSELL FEARN

RETURN TO AKADA

Complete and Unabridged

LINFORD
Leicester

First published in Great Britain

First Linford Edition
published 2010

British Library CIP Data

Fearn, John Russell, *1908 – 1960*.
  Return to Akada.- -(Linford mystery library)
  1. Women, White- -Africa, West- -Fiction.
  2. Geographical myths- -Africa, West- -
  Fiction. 3. Suspense fiction.
  4. Large type books.
  I. Title II. Series
  823.9′12–dc22

  ISBN 978–1–44480–218–4

Published by
F. A. Thorpe (Publishing)
Anstey, Leicestershire
Set by Words & Graphics Ltd.
Anstey, Leicestershire
Printed and bound in Great Britain by
T. J. International Ltd., Padstow, Cornwall
This book is printed on acid-free paper

1

Reunion

The slim, blonde-headed girl in a tropical white costume looked with more than normal interest towards the approaching coastline of West Africa. It was the middle of the afternoon, sizzling hot, with only the molten brass of the sun in the startling blue of the sky. The millionaire's yacht, at the rail of which Rita Perrivale stood, hardly made any breeze as it coursed in gently towards the coastline of lower southern Equatorial Africa. And behind the yacht, at a distance of perhaps a mile, a much larger vessel moved — a tramp steamer.

'You want us to draw in at Loango, Mrs. Perrivale?'

The girl turned quickly at the voice, her grey eyes alight with eagerness. The first mate was standing respectfully nearby in his white drill suit.

1

'No, not into Loango itself, Mr. Crespin. Preferably northwards in the direction of Mayumba. It will make it easier for me. There's a military outpost there from which I can get my bearings.'

'Very good. I'll inform the captain — '

'I think I'd better do it myself. Ask him to come and have a word with me, will you?'

The first mate saluted and departed. Rita took another look at the verdure of the distances, then at the coastline itself, and finally turned away. By the time she had walked the deck to the captain's cabin he had just arrived from the bridge. He opened the door of his cabin and motioned the girl inside to a chair. Then he began to pour out drinks.

'Naturally you'll join me, Mrs. Perrivale?' he asked.

The girl smiled languidly. 'Try and stop me, Captain! I think Africa gets hotter every time I come to it.'

Captain Hart handed over the filled glass and then regarded the girl seriously.

'Of course, madam, it is not really any business of mine, but are you sure you know what you are doing?'

'Quite sure!' Rita's grey eyes met his.

'Forgive me, but it all sounds remarkably fantastic. This story of two white men of immense stature loose in the jungle, twin brothers, and both of them contesting the other for the supremacy of the Dark Continent! Then there is this almost legendary city of Akada with its fabulous treasure of gold and ivory . . . '

'It is all *fact*, Captain Hart: please realise that!' There was a sharpness in Rita's voice. 'How do you suppose I got from one side of Africa to the other, from Zanzibar to Loango, straight across the Congo, without help of *some* kind? That help came from Anjani, a white man, but matured in the jungle. I have returned to Africa because I promised him I would, and because I am going to take on board that tramp steamer we have chartered all the gold and ivory it will carry. My husband would have wished it that way.'

'Quite so,' the captain agreed, subdued. It was by no means the first trip he had made to Africa in the Perrivale luxury yacht, but it was the first time Rita had

3

made it without her husband. A gorilla had slain him in the midst of the earlier ghastly journey to fabulous Akada.

'I am using the millions I have inherited to further the 'hobby' my husband loved,' Rita added simply. 'We will pull in further up the coast between Loango and Mayumba. From there I can soon find the military outpost I want. After that it will not be far to the 'Y'-shaped rock where Anjani promised he would meet me when I returned.'

'And you believe he will, having not the least warning that you are nearing Africa?'

'He will be watching for me. I shall require several men to go ashore with me to the 'Y'-rock. Anjani promised to bring many members of the Untani tribe — by which he was reared — to help move the treasure. In return I am granting the Untani trading rights.'

'I see,' Hart said quietly. 'Very well, madam, I will see to it that we anchor as near as possible to the military post you require. I expect that to be in about two hours.'

And, being a good seaman, the captain

had calculated correctly. A little under two hours later the yacht dropped anchor in an inlet. Before long Rita was seated in a boat, the crew pulling powerfully on the oars.

Once she set foot on the sand Rita looked about her and smiled. It felt good to be back again on the Dark Continent. Not because she had any particular love for the jungle with its myriad terrors and crushing heat, but because it meant she would not now be long separated from Anjani. The nine months she had been absent making preparations for this return had seemed interminable — yet, here she was, with the military outpost only a matter of two miles inshore.

With the members of the crew to protect her she stayed only long enough to identify herself to the outpost's commanding officer, then she continued her journey northwards across flat and dusty terrain. Behind her, motionless in the purple of gathering evening, stood the yacht and the tramp steamer, anchored.

'There,' she said presently, nodding ahead, and first-mate Crespin in charge of the party looked towards a rock with upthrust arms which made it the shape of a 'Y'.

'And that is where you will meet this — white man?' Crespin asked in some amazement.

'If he keeps his promise — and only death would stop him — yes.'

Despite the distance already covered and the flogging heat Rita began to move more swiftly and in another thirty minutes the rock had been gained. Beyond it stretched desert, and beyond that again the wilderness of the mighty jungle.

'Apparently,' Crespin said dryly, looking around him, 'your white friend has forgotten his date, Mrs. Perrivale — '

He broke off, his hand flying to his gun. The men around him also whipped out their weapons and stood tensed and ready. Rita put her hand on the revolver strapped to her waist and then smiled.

Emerging from the cover of the rocks near the dominant 'Y' spur there came a party of ebon-skinned warriors, spears in their hands. But they carried them in an entirely unwarlike fashion, some of them even laid across one shoulder in rifle-style. There were perhaps twenty of them, magnificently muscled, but even so they fell short by several inches of the stature of the white man who came up behind them.

Blankly the members of the yacht's crew stared at him, then mechanically put their guns back in their holsters. He stood a good six-feet-four, with muscle-packed chest and shoulders. Physical strength radiated from every movement he made — yet it was not strength at the expense of looks or intelligence. He was ruggedly handsome, thick blond hair tied back from his powerful features with a thong. Except for a leopard skin loincloth, in which a knife was thrust, he was naked and unarmed, his skin burned to the colour of a Barcelona nut from constant exposure to the African outdoors.

'Anjani!' Rita whispered, scarcely believing. 'Anjani, you kept your promise!'

She hurried forward and the sailors watched in grave interest as the giant swept her from her feet in his great hands, kissed her gently, then set her down again.

'Rita,' he murmured, smiling, his blue eyes bright, 'it has been many moons — too many. I have waited, and waited, but do you not think I speak English well now?'

Rita looked at him in amazement. 'Well? Why, it's — it's uncanny! I gave you the rudiments, I know, but those alone couldn't account for the way you speak now.'

'I found a white man,' he explained simply. 'He was ill — near death. He had sought solitude in the jungle and I came on him by accident. He taught me — all day. Every day . . . Now he is dead.'

'Which makes it so much easier for us to talk,' Rita said. Then she returned to the business on hand, and pointed. 'Those two ships in the distance are mine, the big one to carry the Akada treasure. These men belong to your tribe, I suppose?'

'Yes. All we have to do now is trek to Akada.'

'But not tonight! I have done a lot of walking and I'm tired. The men here have all the equipment for a camp.'

'Of course,' Anjani smiled. 'I never shall remember that you have not my strength and endurance.'

'Well, I should think not!' First Mate Crespin exclaimed. Then he held out his hand, 'Glad to know you, Anjani. Mrs. Perrivale has told all of us a good deal about you.'

Anjani returned the handshake and then turned to the black warriors of the Untani gathered around him.

'Help these men prepare camp,' he ordered, in their own tongue, and without hesitation they obeyed.

They were in the midst of it when the last rays of the sun vanished and the quick tropical night descended. Whilst the camp preparations were going ahead Rita took Anjani on one side in the misty starlight,

'Have you thought any more about my suggestion that you should come to civilization and establish your real identity?' she asked.

'Yes.' Anjani was silent for a while, a massive silhouette against the stars as he sat beside the girl. 'For the sake of being near you, Rita, I would willingly come to civilization — but it is not as simple as that. My twin, Tocoto, is still abroad somewhere and with the jewel of Akada in his possession he can gain mastery over everyone in the jungle. He can do that because the natives are naturally superstitious and Tocoto is wily enough to know it.'

'But what does it matter if he *does* gain the mastery of the tribes? It won't concern you if you are in civilization, will it?'

'*All* the tribes include my own, the Untani,' Anjani answered. 'I cannot allow them to be ruled by Tocoto. I must stay until he is vanquished. I have tried to locate him, but it would have taken too long to do it properly, so I returned here with the Untani warriors to await your return.'

After a brief silence Rita said, 'In a matter of a month, at the longest, I shall be on my way back to England with the tramp steamer loaded. It will seem a pretty empty accomplishment without you beside me. You have no way of dealing with Tocoto in that time and making yourself free to come back with me? It won't be for all time, of course. We'll often come back to Africa to collect more treasure. I don't expect to be able to remove everything at one journey.'

Anjani did not reply. Apparently he was thinking out the matter.

'I think I have a clue as to your identity,' Rita continued. 'When I returned to England I had a detective agency at work tracing an expedition to Africa some twenty years ago. Without going into the details they finally unearthed the fact that a Mark Hardnell and his wife, Ruth, left Zanzibar for the interior about twenty years ago. The woman had been warned by a doctor in Zanzibar not to make the trip as she was due shortly to have a child. There the story ends — but my guess is that twins were born and that you and Tocoto are those twins. Since that expedition was the only one about that time it seems to tie up.'

'Mmmm,' Anjani responded, apparently not very interested. 'I have made my own life, Rita. How it began does not signify — though possibly you are right. Maybe the parents of Tocoto and myself were overtaken by savage tribes and killed, whilst we survived. What does — '

Anjani broke off, his animal senses suddenly alert. He turned his head sharply and looked into the waste of darkness that was the desert. His hand dropped to his knife.

'What's the matter?' Rita asked in surprise, looking about her.

'I heard sounds, not of the night.'

Anjani rose to his feet and stood tensed, like a gigantic statue, Rita still lounging at his feet. Then she gasped in surprise as the — to her — inaudible noise Anjani had detected abruptly took shape in a chorus of war-like yells. Out of the darkness from amidst the scattered rocks at the edge of the desert black figures came hurtling, spears upraised.

'We're being attacked!' Rita shouted hoarsely, clutching hold of Anjani's arm. 'A savage tribe from somewhere . . . '

Anjani hardly needed telling. He flung her down quickly on her face so that the suddenly hurtling spears were not likely to strike her. Chaos hit the camp as, completely outnumbered, the Untani warriors and the yacht's crew fought frantically with the oncoming hordes. It seemed pretty obvious they had been concealed behind the rocks, watching their chance.

Anjani crouched, swaying his body from side to side to dodge the spears that hurtled towards him, and so perfectly coordinated were his actions and so keen his night-sight he escaped harm. Then he leapt into action as the Untani and ship's crew battled savagely, guns exploding and spears whizzing through the darkness.

Leaping suddenly, Anjani brought down the nearest black and drove his knife clean through the warrior's jugular. In an instant he was up again, slamming a steel-hard fist straight into the face of the tribesman bearing down on the recumbent Rita. The native staggered backwards, his neck broken with the terrific impact of the blow.

So far Anjani got, then he realised he had been seized from behind, a forearm under his chin and vice-like fingers striving to tear the knife from his grip. It only took Anjani a moment to discover that his attacker was white, and about the same size as himself.

'Tocoto!' he gasped, and found his knife twisted out of his grip.

Rita, afraid to move, stared fixedly at the two giant white men in the starlight. The melee going on in the half destroyed camp no longer interested her; even the explosion of guns did not startle her. Her whole interest at the moment was centred on the outcome of this meeting of the twins, the first time they had ever locked in combat.

The moment his knife was snatched from him Anjani bent forward suddenly, flinging Tocoto's huge body over his head and crashing him to the ground. Then they were at each other's throats, muscles straining to the limit, each striving desperately to crush the life out of the other.

Rita watched for a moment or two, wincing at the thuds of fists on bone and flesh — then she remembered her revolver and dragged it from its holster.

Twisting round so that she was flat on her face, her firing elbow supported on the ground, she waited for an opportunity — only it never came. Before she could fire a warrior came out of the darkness, tore the gun from her hand, and whirled her to her feet.

She fought frantically to free herself from the black, steel-strong body, but without avail.

'Anjani!' she screamed, as a black hand strove to smother her mouth. 'Anj — '

Anjani heaved, goaded by her cries. He whipped up a blinding uppercut that took his twin clean on the nose and pulped blood out of it. A terrific right to the jaw followed, and another piston blow into the stomach. Without realising it, he had given three punches that Joe Louis might have envied. Tocoto gulped and slewed round drunkenly — and in those seconds Anjani tore free of him and hurtled to the warrior bearing Rita away.

The warrior had to drop the girl to battle with his enemy, but he hardly stood a chance. His head exploded in sparks as a fist crashed into his eye. Another blow flayed a deep cut across his cheek, a third swung him clean off his feet and dropped him six yards away, dazed and helpless. Anjani picked up the warrior's spear, swung it round, then found himself borne to the ground by six warriors in a sudden vengeful rush. There was just nothing he could do against superior numbers and he had to submit as he was bound tightly with thongs about the wrists and ankles. In dumb fury he watched Rita being similarly pinioned and he growled in animal fury as she was flung unceremoniously beside him.

Tocoto came up in the starlight, rubbing his blood-smeared nose with the back of his hand. With a simple call he withdrew the rest of his warriors from the camp, leaving behind many dead and mortally injured white men and the scattered survivors of the Untani, far too battered to fight any more.

'If you doubt, Anjani, who is lord of jungle, you now know,' Tocoto said, in the tribal tongue. 'Tocoto lord because I have jewel of Akada. The drums have told all the tribes that I am Tocoto the Mighty.'

'Not while I live,' Anjani snarled back.

'Anjani and white woman soon die,' Tocoto retorted. 'Die as sacrifices to the Banwui tribe — Tocoto's tribe! Mantamiza cheated once, but not again. Tribal god demands vengeance, and shall have it. Tocoto watch what you do and gather tribes to aid him. When time was ripe, Tocoto struck — and destroyed those who help you. Only one lord of jungle, Anjani, and that is Tocoto the Mighty.'

Rita, not understanding the jargon, looked from one to the other in the tropical starlight, trying vainly to gather what was going to happen. She found out quickly enough when a warrior, at Tocoto's command, picked her up like a child and slung her over his shoulder. Four more warriors lifted Anjani's great body between them, then the victorious tribesmen began marching with Tocoto at their head.

Just what had been left behind at the camp neither Anjani nor Rita knew. Certainly few who could be of help. The score of Untani warriors had been sadly depleted and the white men had all but been wiped out. For Anjani and Rita the journey on which they were carried seemed endless, and filled with torture. The only liberty Tocoto permitted in the few halts which were made were for the rope-thongs to be loosened a little and food and water, in meagre supply provided — but in the main it was a jolting journey on the shoulders of the warriors, through the desert first, then in the midst of the jungle with its myriad dangers and saturating heat.

It was a trip that took nearly a week, and at the end of it Rita was more dead than alive. Anjani was blond-bearded and grim, his daily shave with his hunting knife having been prevented. At the journey's end Rita looked with bleared eyes at the stockade gateway of the Banwui tribe's village with the hideous effigy of Mantamiza, the tribal god, rearing at its far end amidst the mud-huts. She licked her parched lips and gave Anjani a hopeless look.

He was not looking at her, or the village; instead he was viewing the sky where it peeped through the lofty treetops. The air was leaden with heat and stiflingly still. Yet the sun was not shining. There was a leaden yellow haze over the blueness.

Anjani did not say what thought had crossed his mind, but Rita fancied she saw the ghost of a smile amidst his magnificent yellow beard and moustache, then her arms were seized again and she was bundled forward across the dusty centre of the village and finally into a mud-hut. Anjani was flung after her and the wood and raffia door closed. But outside it remained the shadows of three natives on guard.

'Won't they even give us water?' Rita whispered, her tongue nearly too swollen to permit of speech.

'I doubt it,' Anjani muttered. 'They have no reason to be merciful since they mean to burn us to death at nightfall. It would not be sensible to make the victim comfortable, would it?'

Rita did not answer. Half sobbing she flung herself down on the filthy dry grass of the hut. Anjani crouched and looked at her. Her once trim white costume was torn to shreds with thorns and under-growth. Scratched white flesh showed here and there and her blonde hair was an unkempt tangle.

Anjani reached down, cupped a huge arm underneath her shoulders, then raised her. Her head lolled against his broad chest.

'Do not give in too soon, little one,' he murmured. 'There may yet be a chance.'

'Such as?' Rita asked hopelessly.

'We shall see. Anjani, jungle-wise, can read signs that may come to pass. Tocoto is master because he has a jewel, but if natives are superstitious in one thing, then they are in another. I shall try my last trick tonight . . . '

Rita did not answer. She was too bone-weary and thirsty to even think.

'Tocoto must have kept close track of me and gathered tribes to aid him,' Anjani mused presently. 'It is only to be expected. There will never be room for both of us in the jungle.'

Rita was hardly listening. Finally she took refuge in sleep, still with her head on Anjani's shoulder. He remained motionless lest he disturb her. As he had expected, no water or nourishment was brought and the guards remained outside the doorway. Once or twice Anjani speculated on the possibilities of attacking them, and then changed his mind. Single-handed, nimble and powerful as he was, he could probably have made his escape, but not with Rita to look after as well. So he licked his parched lips and waited — and waited.

Towards the close of the hot, sultry afternoon preparations began for the festival of nightfall. Anjani could see part of the proceedings through a crack in the ancient wall of the hut, and they followed the usual pattern. Two stakes set near to the evergrowing pile of brushwood, the effigy of Mantamiza near at hand and, behind it, a tall stump on which reposed something dull red and faceted. It was not particularly big and Anjani recognised it as the jewel of Akada, set in a place of honour.

Rita awoke at nightfall, her voice failing her through lack of water. She remained in Anjani's grasp, staring dully through the crack in the wall and listening to the gathering rumble of the drums. The way she felt she did not particularly care if she did die. Thirst was fast killing her in any case.

Night itself seemed to come sooner than usual with heavy lowering clouds. The air remained motionless so that not a leaf stirred and the maddening beat of the drums was carried with reverberating echoes. Outside the warriors were dancing. Directly underneath the jewel of Akada and Mantamiza Tocoto was seated in a rush chair, surveying the proceedings, a grim-faced white giant, amidst his black followers.

Then, suddenly, the door of the prison hut flew open and Anjani found himself seized by four massive warriors. He stood little chance against them and was bundled fiercely outside. Two remaining warriors grabbed the half unconscious Rita between them and dragged her to her feet. Stumbling, dazed, she was forced across the dusty clearing in the centre of the village until one of the stakes had been reached. She drew back in horror before the naked blaze of the crackling fire, only to be forced onwards again, her back finally coming up hard against the stake assigned to her. In a matter of moments she had been bound to it, her head lolling. Near to her, Anjani was bound to his own pillar, but he remained erect, looking bitterly towards his twin on the seat beneath the effigy.

Presently Tocoto rose and held up his hand. The noise of the drums and the *m'deup* dance faded into silence. The quiet was uncanny, resting on both the village and the surrounding jungle. Nothing moved for a while and there was a vast oppression in the air.

'Tocoto speak few words before sacrifice!' Tocoto looked about him and at the sound of his voice, though she could not understand what he was saying, Rita raised her head. Her face was greasy from the heat of the fire, her hair tangled about her head. Her cracked lips and tongue showed just how much thirst was corroding the life out of her.

'Anjani great danger to all tribes,' Tocoto continued. 'Tocoto rule, not Anjani, because I have the power of the jewel which gives us lordship over our enemies — '

'I challenge that!' Anjani interrupted, and immediately the warriors and their mates looked at him in surprise.

'You *dare* to challenge Tocoto the Mighty?' Tocoto roared.

'I do. Jewel of Akada gives you great power, you say — power over the gods of evil, power even over Mantamiza. I have greater power and can command the gods of rain to come to my aid if need be!'

'You have no power,' Tocoto shouted back. 'Tocoto alone is master — '

'Try and burn me and the white woman as sacrifices to Mantamiza and the rain gods will destroy you,' Anjani cried.

There was a momentary hesitation amongst the natives and the fuming of Tocoto did not budge them either. Inherently superstitious they were faced with two masters — the one who claimed absolute authority because of the jewel he possessed, and the other who swore he could bring the rain gods to his aid.

In the pause Anjani looked hopefully above him. He had known from the very start that a violent tropical storm was threatening: all the signs had been there ever since arriving in the village. The point was, how soon would it reach flashpoint?

'On with the dance!' Tocoto roared. 'Mantamiza grows impatient! Into the fire with them! First the woman and then the man ... But not too quickly. Let them taste the flames first. Remember, Mantamiza was cheated last time. This time he will like to play with his victims!'

Immediately there was a rush of warriors to the stake holding Rita. She screamed helplessly for Anjani to aid her as the stake began to rock back and forth, then at last it was lifted out of its socket and on to the shoulders of four of the warriors. Face down, held by the ropes, Rita felt herself being carried to the flames.

'Hold!' Anjani thundered. 'The rain gods forbid! Look up, you misguided fools — look up!'

The warriors hesitated, then they obeyed, which was one sure way of making them feel raindrops spattering onto their faces. At almost the same instant, to Anjani's profound thankfulness, a fork of lightning ripped the sky and thunder exploded with shattering violence over the village.

'The rain gods will destroy you if you dare burn me or the white woman!' Anjani yelled, rain now pelting down hard. 'Put the woman down. Release her!'

'Do not obey him — !' Tocoto waved his arms frantically.

But at the moment the signs were all on the side of the rain gods, which was the only thing the natives understood. With rain sweeping down in clouds and thunder cannonading overhead they were quite convinced that Anjani, not Tocoto, was the man to be feared. Hastily they put Rita down and cut her free, dragging her to her feet. She turned her face to the sky and drank in the precious drops that poured down her face.

Then the warriors turned to Anjani, their keen knives cutting at his thongs. Tocoto watched in impotent fury for a moment or two, then realising that he had lost the battle — and that it might go ill for him too if the natives were so minded — he turned, grabbed the great Jewel of Akada, and vanished in the darkness away from the rapidly extinguishing fire. But Anjani saw him go, illumined by the flashes of lightning, and the moment he was released he dashed across to where Rita was still on her knees, drinking in the rain.

'Come — quickly,' Anjani told her, and with a hand under her arm he pulled her along beside him. This time she moved more quickly, already revived by the water, the coolness, and the fact that she had escaped death.

In a moment or two she and Anjani were in the jungle. The lightning blazed eerily for a moment, then thunder crashed down on the darkness that followed. There was a wind now, bending the treetops and sending clouds of water downwards, feeding the baked earth and vegetation. Jungle dwellers, startled by the storm, were keeping up a ceaseless commotion and scurrying.

Finally, after travelling perhaps a quarter of a mile into the forest with Rita stumbling beside him, Anjani came to a halt. Rita looked at him as a more distant flash of lightning penetrated the foliage for a moment.

'Where are we going?' she questioned. 'Following a trail back to — to where we came from?' Her voice quieted as she remembered the great distance that lay between them and the ships at anchor on the coastline.

'I was trying to follow Tocoto and settle things between us once and for all,' Anjani answered. 'The storm has upset things, though, and everything is lost. I can't follow a trail in this, and by night. We must shelter and try again by daylight.'

'But what about the natives? Won't they follow us?'

'I don't think so. They believe that I am the master to be obeyed because the storm broke just in time to make my threats come true. So they won't follow because they won't dare. Later, though, Tocoto will talk them round again. He will have to, or completely lose all the authority he has gained. As for us, we may as, well find somewhere to rest for the night.'

It did not take him long to discover a comparative dry spot in the undergrowth, to which he helped Rita and bade her lie down. Then above her he constructed a roof of broad and dripping leaves that broke the full force of the still pelting rain. Not that the water mattered. It was a relief from the crushing heat that normally reigned in this wilderness.

Even with the shelter constructed Anjani was not satisfied. He departed on a brief investigation of his own, to Rita's horror, then when he returned he had an armful of coconuts. The milk from them and the solid interior was sufficient to provide a temporary meal.

Almost immediately afterwards, secure again in the thought that Anjani was beside her, Rita fell asleep once more. When she awakened again she was alone, the hot sun glinting through the treetops and her remnants of clothes dried to her mud-caked body. She stirred stiffly and looked about her in alarm.

'Anjani!' she cried frantically. 'Anjani!'

She scrambled to her feet and blundered out of the leaf-shelter, then to her relief she beheld Anjani in the centre of the little clearing, busy cooking some small animal over a fire. He had even prepared plates made of leaves and had poured fruit juice into the hollow coconut shells. In fact, quite an appetising breakfast was at hand,

Smiling with relief, Rita settled down and watched him at work, the sunlight gleaming from his mighty shoulders, his muscles rippling with every move he made. He took a glance at her and then grinned, rubbing his ill-shaven chin. His beard he had removed by singeing.

'White people are not supposed, so you say, to wear as little as the natives,' he commented.

Rita looked down at herself and sighed. She barely had enough clothes left to cover her, but somehow it did not seem to matter. The sun was warm to her still tired body and its return after the wet of the night seemed to be bringing new life back to her.

'Only one thing for it,' she decided, as she started upon the meal he had prepared. 'Another vegetable dress. When

I get back to civilization, if ever, I should think I might start a fashion in wearing leaves instead of cloth.'

Anjani smiled broadly once again. 'When we get back to civilization,' he corrected.

Rita looked at him quickly, her grey eyes wide. 'You mean you've actually decided to come back with me?'

'I have. The more I am with you the more I know I can never do without you. My life and yours are bound up in each other.'

'But what about Tocoto?'

'Before I go I shall destroy him. It will not be difficult now he is abroad in the jungle and afraid of those he formerly ruled. I shall find him this very day.'

'Unarmed?' Rita asked quietly,

Anjani glanced down at the blank space upon his loincloth where his knife usually rested. He shrugged his broad shoulders.

'I have fingers and muscles, and I shall be fighting a man and not an animal. I shall win — because I must.'

'Then when that is done, all we have to do is go back to Akada, get the treasure, and then — sail for home?'

'Just that.'

Rita forgot her meal for the moment and leaned forward, bringing her arms about Anjani's neck. His arm encircled her slim waist, and for a moment they were silent. These were the moments Rita loved best, with his mighty frame so close to her, always there to protect her —

A sound made Anjani glance up. Rita did not trouble because she was quite happy where she was, but as she felt Anjani's muscles tense she too looked across the clearing. And paradise seemed to evaporate instantly.

Tocoto was standing only a few yards away, his knife in his hand, frozen hatred in his handsome face.

2

Rita abducted

'Before I return, Anjani, to recover the tribe leadership which you destroyed for me last night,' Tocoto said, 'I am going to settle the issue which stands between us. So often you have looked for me: this time I have looked for you, and found you! And the white woman! Maybe when I have disposed of you she will make a useful mate for no other reason than that her skin is white.'

Whilst he had been speaking, Tocoto had been coming forward slowly at a half-crouch, his knife ready in his hand Anjani remained exactly where he was, half recumbent with Rita nestled against him. Her wide grey eyes followed every one of Tocoto's movements and it was hard for her to realise that she was not looking at Anjani himself.

Then suddenly Anjani got to his feet

and motioned to Rita.

'Better to stay on the side of the clearing, Rita while this issue is settled,' he said. 'You didn't understand what Tocoto said just now, of course, but this is the final battle between us for supremacy.'

Rita got up slowly and backed away, her eyes on the two men as they circled each other.

'Your having no knife will not make it any the easier for you, Anjani,' Tocoto commented, grinning.

'I do not need one for so puny an antagonist.'

That punctured Tocoto's ego com-pletely, just as Anjani had hoped it would; He suddenly lunged forward, his knife raised to swing it straight to Anjani's breast. Anjani saw the blow coming and with perfect timing gripped Tocoto's knife-wrist as it came down and twisted savagely. Tocoto clung on to his knife but twirled off balance, tripping afterwards over Anjani's outflung foot and then landing on his back.

Immediately Anjani was on top of him, his steel-hard fingers gripping his twin's throat. Tocoto brought his knife down swiftly towards Anjani's back and he gasped a little as the blade sliced his side and drew blood. He retaliated by suddenly moving one of his hands from Tocoto's throat, bunching it into a fist, and slamming it down into the face in front of him.

Tocoto yelped with the pain of the blow, heaved up, and flung Anjani from him. Anjani rolled a few feet and scrambled up, jabbing a straight left into Tocoto's stomach, as he came hurtling forward with his knife. The impact of the punch doubled him up, and as he doubled Anjani seized his knife-arm and wrenched it furiously backwards until the knife dropped. He stooped to pick it up, and received an up-jerked knee in his face, which felt as though it had smashed his nose. With a gasp he tottered, and then a sledgehammer blow to the jaw flattened him on his back. Then, knife in hand again, Tocoto was on top of him, striving with all the huge strength he possessed to bring the blade down either on Anjani's throat or heart.

But Anjani was strong too, his arms as straight as ramrods, and corded with muscle. Fiercely though he struggled, Tocoto could not break down that up-thrusting strain — so he abruptly switched his tactics and swung up his arm preparatory to driving the blade down into Anjani's stomach. Anjani anticipated the move, jack-knifed his legs, then thrust them outwards with all his power. They caught Tocoto in the midriff, pitched him into the air, then dropped him heavily several feet away.

Anjani was up immediately, this time attacking Tocoto from the rear. He jumped on his back and locked one massive forearm under Tocoto's jaw, tearing backwards with all his power. Tocoto squirmed and shifted helplessly, his hand wildly flaying the air with the knife, then Anjani's free hand clamped down, twisted the wrist devilishly, and tore the knife free.

Tocoto did the only thing he could: he deliberately made himself fall backwards so he was on top of Anjani, back-first. In a moment he had remedied this, twisting round, both his hands gripping Anjani's wrist as he tried to wield the knife. The steel grip on the tendons of his hand made him drop the weapon, but though he had lost it he did not allow Tocoto to get it. Instead he seized him by the throat and whirled him over. For a moment or two it was first one then the other on top, each grunting and gasping under a hail of smashing blows to face and body.

As he struggled Anjani fancied he heard Rita scream once or twice, but paid little attention, assuming that it was his welfare with which she was concerned. Knowing exactly what he intended to do to Tocoto before he was finished he concentrated solely on the job of absorbing blows and hitting back violently, until an opening showed itself — then, as he rolled sideways to avoid a downward punch he caught sight of something. Rita, struggling helplessly in the grip of a hairy man-like creature, that was bearing her out of the clearing. Almost immediately the great beast had vanished, and Rita with him,

Anjani was so astounded he could not

believe it for the moment, and those few seconds off-guard gave Tocoto his chance. His hands flashed down and gripped Anjani's throat with deadly power, squeezing tighter, and tighter still. As he fought to tear the hands away Anjani realised one thing — Rita had been abducted by a bull ape. The beast, evidently more interested in her than the fighting white giants, had swept her up and left the men to their own devices —

The fate of Rita was the one thing in Anjani's mind at the moment. His battle with Tocoto counted for nothing. He had got to get free to help Rita — So, suddenly, he redoubled his efforts and by sheer muscular force tore away the hands at his throat. He surged to his feet and whipped up a devastating uppercut that caught Tocoto beautifully on the point of the jaw. He stumbled back on his heels, to gasp and grunt as two more punches smashed into his nose and mouth. Streaked with blood he dropped on his knees, then, when a hammer blow descended on the back of his neck at the base of the skull he flattened out, temporarily stunned, or even dead: Anjani did not wait to find out.

He whipped up the fallen knife, jammed it in his loincloth thong, then plunged into the forest where the bull ape had vanished. For a second or two he listened and, hearing nothing, vaulted up to the nearest tree, climbed it with the agility of a cat, and then began speeding through the vegetation, branch to branch. Never had he moved so fast: never had the need been more urgent, but his task was rendered doubly difficult because the ape had apparently also taken to the treetops, which made following his trail difficult.

Actually the ape was perhaps a mile away from Anjani to the south, Rita was held tightly against him with one enormous arm. So far she had suffered no hurt, but she was mortally afraid of the shaggy beast, particularly when his red eyes under the sloping, narrow cranium looked down at her and he bared his fighting fangs for a moment.

In size the ape was not full-grown and, had Rita been well versed in Jungle-lore, not particularly dangerous either. It had reached the age when it played more than it fought and anything new attracted it immediately, just as a child might be attracted. Rita, alive and white-skinned, was a novelty and worth taking, which was why she squirmed helplessly in the grip of the shaggy arm, or beat her fists on the barrel of a chest. None of which made any difference. The ape continued to grip her round the waist, her legs flying free and her hands pounding at him incessantly.

The monkeys chattered noisily as the ape progressed and they scattered out of the way of their giant brother. Just where the journey was going to end Rita did not know. It seemed to last an interminable time, but finally the beast dropped from the trees to the ground and hurried swiftly over a stretch of rocky terrain existing like a blind spot in the verdure. Here there were rocky cliffs and harsh, arid landscape soaked in the blazing sun. So finally across a narrow, dusty gulch, then into the mouth of a big cave.

Here was evidently the ape's home, or

else its own secret hiding place. In any event the mighty arm loosened and Rita slid to the rocky floor. Instantly she backed away, her eyes wide in fright, as the ape grunted in satisfaction and towered over her. His red eyes pinned her — then he began to amble up and down on his short legs, knuckles touching the floor. His endeavour, though it meant nothing to the frightened girl, was to purely exhibit his prowess and physique, as he might to the female of his own species.

Rita's only reaction was to crouch by the further shadowy wall of the big cave and look fearfully about her for a way of escape. She screamed with horror when at last the ape, realising she was taking no notice, ceased his strutting and came forward swiftly. His big paw lashed out, seized her wrist, and forced her to his body with irresistible strength. She lashed out with her free hand and drove deep nail gouges down the beast's face. He growled with the pain and rising fury — then hit back. The blow, luckily for Rita, missed her head and struck her shoulder instead. Even as it was she went spinning against the wall and then slid to the floor, dazed and feeling as if her shoulder were broken.

From this point onwards she felt as a mouse might in the hands of a cat. Being only a plaything, to be later discarded, the ape picked her up and put her down again constantly. She screamed with pain and lashed and kicked when he lifted her solely by her hair with one hand, only to toss her away again after a moment or two. In dropping, however, she found herself on loose stone, which had fallen from the roof and this afforded her first feeling of confidence. She picked one of the small rocks up and hurled it viciously. It struck the ape a glancing blow on the side of the head and it turned in snarling anger, his fangs bared. So Rita threw again and yet again, with all her force.

It was about the worst thing she could have done. The beast was no longer playing: he was incensed and vindictive. Growling with fury he dived at her, catching her ankle as she tried desperately to squirm out of reach behind the rocks at the rear of the cave. Instantly she was pulled out of hiding, her bare arms scratched by the loose stone over which she was dragged.

Just what the ape planned to do with her, Rita did not know, nor, to her relief, did she have the chance to find out, for there came a sudden interruption as a giant white man, knife between his teeth, jumped quickly through the cave opening and looked about him.

The ape released Rita's ankle and she lay on the floor looking in tearful thankfulness towards Anjani. He gave her a glance, then circled slowly as, rumbling with fury at the interruption, the bull ape prepared to charge at him.

Anjani was wary. He knew exactly the habits of the jungle creatures and just when this swaggering young bull would make a lunge — and he guessed right, timing his own movement accordingly. The instant the ape charged, Anjani sidestepped and retracted his right arm. He slammed it forward again at the instant the ape passed him, driving his fist with deadly force straight into the ape's stomach. He gulped and howled with fury at the pain and lack of wind, by which time Anjani had swung around and vaulted onto the shaggy back.

One arm under the ape's chin in an unbreakable armlock, he used his free hand to wield his knife, driving it deep, again and again into the vast chest. Three times he stabbed and the ape screamed and lunged with pain and terror to dislodge the white demon from his back. Then the fourth blow went true, straight to the hilt in the savage heart. The ape's screeching died in its throat and Anjani whipped himself clear, knife included, so he would not be pinned under the heavy body. It crashed over on its face and remained motionless, except for reactionary twitching, as muscles and nerves began to die.

'Anjani,' Rita whispered, staggering up as he came over to her. 'The times you save me . . . The dangers I keep making you face!'

'Dangers?' Anjani glanced towards the dead ape and gave a grim smile. 'Not much danger from that, little one. He was only a young one. The danger comes from the giant gorilla, like the one which half-killed me last time you were in Africa — You are not hurt?'

'No, no. I suppose he — he was playing. But it was mighty rough play while it lasted. How did you find me? What happened to Tocoto?'

'I had to leave him and follow you. He is still alive, and as such a danger. I will find him again . . . To find you was not so difficult. From the disturbed chattering of the monkeys I could work out which way you had been taken.' Rita did not answer. Anjani's arm about her, they reached the cave mouth and then paused. The girl asked a question.

'Which way now, Anjani?'

He became thoughtful. 'Most of the warriors I had gathered from my tribe were wiped out in Tocoto's attack. It is no use returning to Akada until we have more who can help us. I think we should return to my own village.'

'Just as you say,' Rita assented, content to leave it to him to do as he thought best — so they began moving, sometimes through the treetops, sometimes on the jungle floor, Anjani always alert for and circumventing any danger which showed itself.

Rita had no idea which direction was taken since, to her, all sides of the jungle looked alike, but Anjani, knowing the wilderness like the palm of his hand, found his way through it to the point where the village of the Untani tribe lay, a fairly extensive kraal surrounded by the usual stockade. It was three days later when it was reached, towards mid-afternoon, and there hung about it an unaccustomed, solemn stillness.

Anjani came to a halt and surveyed, his face showing that he was puzzled.

'Queer,' he mused, as Rita glanced up at him in surprise. 'Usually at this hour the kraal is busy.'

He moved on again, a little faster this time, Rita clinging to his arm. They entered the wide-open gates of the stockade and then came to a stop once more, stunned by the scene of utter desolation and massacre that lay before them.

On every hand, motionless bodies of men and women were lying, some with assegais still impaling them others tied to the surrounding trees with vine. Apparently every one was dead. The mud and thatch habitations themselves were practically destroyed, most of them burned to dead ash.

'What's — what's happened?' Rita asked at last, blankly. 'It looks as if there has been an attack by a savage tribe, or something! It — ' She broke off, her eye caught by a distant movement. 'Look over there! Somebody still alive, trying to crawl along the ground.'

Anjani nodded and hurried forward. The chocolate-brown figure that Rita had noticed was that of a youngish woman, one far less black than the rest of the tribe.

'Limina!' Anjani cried, as he reached her, and he raised her head and shoulders in one arm.

Limina smiled faintly, the tired, dead smile of one not far from the finish. Across the breast of the coarse cotton weave dress she was wearing, blood was still thickly streaked.

'Anjani,' she whispered back. 'Limina always love Anjani. Now too late . . . '

Anjani nodded sympathetically as she spoke in the tribal tongue. Limina, with white blood somewhere in her makeup, had always been the one who had believed she would one day mate with him, until Miambo, the head of the tribe, had forbidden it.

'What happened?' Anjani demanded. 'Who caused all this devastation?'

'Tocoto and many warriors. They came upon us without warning. I think they looked for you and the white woman. They killed everybody, including Miambo, the wise one.'

Anjani was silent, the lines tightening about his mouth. To hear of losing Miambo, the wise old tribal chief who had been like a father to him was bitter indeed.

'Some — some less hurt than others,' Limina finished, closing her eyes. 'I — one of them, but now — I — I am dying, Anjani.'

'When did all this happen?' Anjani questioned.

'Just — after dawn today.'

There were other questions Anjani would have liked to ask but there was no opportunity. Limina relaxed and became silent, her head lolling to one side.

'What did she say?' Rita asked. 'I heard the name Tocoto, but the rest I could not understand.'

Anjani gave her the story as briefly as possible, then he lifted Limina's dead body in this arms and carried it across; to the remains of the dwelling which had been hers. Gently he laid her on the matting floor within. When he came out into the sunlight again his face was grimmer than Rita had ever seen it.

'This alters things, little one,' he said, looking at her. 'No men are left of the Untani, beyond the scant few who may have escaped at Akada, to move the treasure from the storehouses. Tocoto has wiped everybody out, because they were connected with me, I suppose — even including poor Miambo, the wise one. For that alone I would have had to exact vengeance.'

Rita looked a little puzzled. 'I don't

quite see how he did it. I thought the tribes had outcast him after you had proved yourself the supposed lord of rain and thunder.'

'Evidently he talked himself back into favour again. It would not be so difficult for him with the sunlight back again and my influence removed. That jewel of his has a tremendous effect on the native mind . . . ' Anjani clenched his fists. 'For us, at least, the way is clear. I must hound Tocoto out of Africa or else kill him. This attack on my tribe is the worst thing he has ever done, and is pure viciousness. We will rest here awhile, use what food there may be, and then start to find Tocoto. There is every reason now why I should be avenged upon him . . . '

★   ★   ★

Anjani was right in his assumption that Tocoto had talked himself back into favour with the Banwui — his own tribe, but he had only managed it by promising immense conquests and the overlordship by the Banwui of all the tribes, near and far. And, to implement his promise, Tocoto had wasted no time in starting on an orgy of destruction to prove how absolute was his power,

Being wily, he worked with a double objective. With a picked score or so of Banwui warriors he was now on his way through the jungle, carrying the Jewel of Akada with him in a leather pouch supported by a thong about his neck. On the way wherever he felt he could win the advantage he gave orders for kraals to be attacked, and added the survivors — awed by his power — to his own small 'safari'. Thuswise, as he went, he gained the necessary labour he knew he would need when he reached Akada.

He had no particular reason for stealing the treasure of Akada since he had no conception of civilised values, but he did realise that Anjani was probably abroad somewhere in the jungle and that, sooner or later, he might make an attempt to obtain the Akada treasure for himself. Tocoto's only thought was to remove the gold and ivory and so forestall him. At a later date some trader might buy in ornaments and other forms of barter from the Banwui tribe. On the other hand, Anjani might he dead in his search for Rita and the ape that had stolen her. Tocoto did not particularly care either way, but he certainly meant making sure that nobody else got the Akada treasure.

At the present moment, whilst Anjani and Rita were recovering from the shock of discovering the ravaged Untani village, Tocoto was four miles to the north of it and progressing steadily with his army of natives in the direction of distant Akada. He was feeling particularly pleased with himself. He had succeeded in disposing of practically every member of the accursed tribe that had reared his brother. True, he had lost some men on his own side, but that did not signify in the least. He still had thirty men with him and would pick up more as fresh villages were reached and wiped out as a proof of his ruthless domination.

And, also only a few miles from Untani, but completely lost in the depths of the mighty forest, a party of white men picked their way. There were perhaps ten of them, comprising what had remained of the ship's crew after the Banwui tribe had attacked them at the coast, reinforced by others from the yacht and steamer and commanded by first-mate Crespin, who had escaped the Banwui onslaught with nothing worse than a gashed shoulder.

'More I see of this, Mr. Crespin, the more I think we're a bunch of damned fools,' one of the men said at last, pushing his rifle back on the shoulder strap impatiently. 'To try and find Mrs. Perrivale and Anjani in this lot is like trying to find the needle in the haystack. Anyway, they're probably dead by now.'

'I begin to think you're right.' Crespin pushed the back of his hand over his sweat-drenched face. 'Three days and more we've been prowling about in this stuff and not found a single clue. As the compass shows we're heading north-wards, we presumably head southwards when we want to return to the coast.'

'I think we should, right now,' another of the party said, and this brought Crespin to a halt. He looked about him on the weary, sweat-stained men, sun-helmets pushed onto the backs of their heads.

'I know how you feel about it, boys,' Crespin said. 'It seems a waste of time and a needless exposure to danger on our part — but as long as we have provisions enough and to spare and can hold out we should go on looking. We are the only ones who can possibly save Mrs. Perrivale.'

'But what the hell's the use, sir?' one of the men snapped. 'By this time that tribe who took them off will have torn them to bits, or burned them, or something. We haven't an earthly chance in this forest — and the deeper we go into it the less chance we stand of ever finding our way back. I'm no coward and I'd like to help Mrs. Perrivale as much as possible, but we've also got ourselves to think of.'

Crespin tightened his lips for a moment. 'If those natives Anjani brought with him hadn't deserted us we might have stood a chance with them as guides. Only six of them survived, I know, but they would have known how to find a way through — ' Crespin paused, listened intently, then gently loosed his rifle from his shoulder. At the same moment the other men made ready too, catching the sounds in the undergrowth. At first they expected an animal would appear, then they recognised the thudding of machetes against vegetation and looked at one another expectantly.

'Hold your ground,' Crespin instructed. 'If we're up against a bunch of natives we might learn something. I understand most of the tribal tongues — '

He had no opportunity to say any more for at that moment a party of natives hacked their way into the small clearing in which the white party stood. They stopped dead, then glanced behind them in uncertainty. In another moment Tocoto came into view, and he too paused in surprise. His hand dropped to the new hunting knife in his loincloth.

'Anjani!' one of the men exclaimed in delight. 'The very man we're looking for!'

Since Tocoto did not understand the language he made no response, but he gathered from the way his hand was shaken up and down that a welcome was intended. He eyed the party narrowly, recognising some of them as those who had been attacked on the coast at his orders.

The white men were not sure whether they were dealing with Anjani or Tocoto, chiefly because they had only seen Tocoto in the dimness of the night — which had failed to pick out the scar on his arm that was his one distinction from his twin. The other lay in his cotton-weave loincloth, whereas Anjani wore a leopard skin, but this detail was something none of the men, not even Crespin, had noticed — again because it had been dark when they had seen Tocoto who might have been quite similarly attired for all they had time to see.

The test lay in whether this particular white giant could talk English fairly well, as Anjani had done, and Crespin wasted no time in putting it to the test.

'We're looking for Mrs. Perrivale, Anjani. Where is she?'

Tocoto did not reply; instead he spoke

to the natives gathered about him in their own tongue.

'These white men are friends of Anjani, your great enemy. And my great enemy, too. But we will not kill them because of that. They can be useful in helping us move the treasure of Akada.'

The natives nodded and grinned at each other. The white men waited, not saying anything — but Crespin was tight-lipped and watchful. Possessing a knowledge of most of the tribal tongues of the Dark Continent he had not found it particularly hard to interpret what Tocoto had said, and he knew exactly whom he was dealing with and how dubious were the immediate prospects.

'Whatever happens, do as this big fellow says,' he ordered, looking at his colleagues. 'We've run into trouble. This isn't the one we want, but the one who attacked us. I'm not using his name in case he picks something up from it. We'll try and work something out later. At the moment, with all these men with him, he has more than an advantage.'

Tocoto had pricked up his ears

considerably during this lengthy statement, but failing to interpret a word of it he merely ended by looking suspicious. But not for long. With a jerk of his head he signalled two of his black warriors and gave them orders.

'Keep the whites going ahead of us. They may be dangerous. Take their weapons from them.'

Immediately Crespin found his rifle and revolver taken, but he made no protest because he did not wish to take the risk. In silence, grim-faced, the other white men gave up their weapons also. It seemed about the worst thing that could have befallen them for them to walk right into the arms of the very man they most sought to avoid.

And, during the jungle trek which they realised by now must end at Akada, they had further proof of Tocoto's power over the natives. Whenever one of them became rebellious it was enough for Tocoto to remove the big blood-red jewel from the pouch about his neck to restore order immediately. And the more he watched these incidents and the effect on the natives the more Crespin thought about them.

If he could only seize that jewel somehow and use it for his own ends, what might he not accomplish . . .

3

Mea

After spending a few hours in the devastated Untani kraal, Rita, resting after a meal of native food, and Anjani — after burying the bodies — fashioning a small cradle from strong, pliable saplings, they both got on the move again. This time Rita found herself transported within the cradle, bound to Anjani's broad back by thongs. It made his movements less restricted as he flew through the treetops seeking the first clue that would help him pick up the trail of Tocoto.

It was late evening when he learned — indirectly — from the disturbed chattering of the ever-observant monkeys which way the trail lay. Immediately Anjani turned southwards, Rita's arms about his neck as she sat in the 'cradle', and flung himself with vengeful speed through the foliage and across dizzying abysses. Probably he would have picked up the trail fairly quickly had not another of the tropical storms suddenly broken.

It seemed only a matter of moments before the swiftly clouded sky became ablaze with whip-lashing lightning and the thunder cannonaded amidst the rain. There was danger at the treetop heights so Anjani descended swiftly to the ground and pushed and cut his way through the dripping vegetation, Rita running beside him with her nearly non-existent clothes plastered to her slender form.

But, as in all storms, trails disappeared as the rain altered the configuration of leaves and under-grass. By the time the evening sun was sullenly breaking through the cloud rifts Anjani realised he was far from the spot he had hoped for.

'We've turned aside somewhere,' he told the girl finally. 'And it's going to be difficult to try and interpret the chattering of disturbed monkeys again. They'll stay in shelter, scared by the storm — I don't recognise that,' he finished, and pointed through the trees.

Rita looked where he indicated and beheld a tall cliff of white rock with bluish veins running through it. At this point the jungle had ceased and the terrain had become rocky, leading down into a boulder-strewn valley with the mighty cliff face beyond.

'It looks to me like the spot where that ape took me,' she said at length. 'Or else very like it.'

'It's not the same spot,' Anjani responded, 'otherwise I would have recognised it. No, it's one of those barren places you find occasionally in the wilderness, and it also shows us how far we are off our course. We'd better — '

Anjani stopped as he half turned to re-enter the jungle vastness. Without a sound, so quietly indeed that even his animal quickness had not detected it, a group of strangely painted black warriors had appeared. There were at least twenty of them and they had deployed themselves in a circle so that they now came also from the concealment of rocks on the valley side. In a matter of a few moments Anjani and Rita found themselves surrounded.

Puzzled, Anjani studied the warriors intently. They did not belong to any tribe he could place, and they were also much less in stature than the average native. The shields they carried were exceptionally ornamental, with lines of pure silver and gold running through them. It seemed fantastic, but the heads of the spears they held so menacingly were of black ivory and the shaft white ivory. In itself each single spear would have been worth a small fortune in the outer world.

'Who are you?' Anjani asked at last, in his own tongue — and received no answer. So he tried others, until at last he discovered one that was evidently understandable, though not very clearly.

'You invade Monango territory,' the leader of the natives explained fiercely. 'Chieftainess not allow strangers in Monango region.'

'Chieftainess?' Anjani repeated in surprise. '*What* Chieftainess?'

'Her Terrible Highness, Mea, High Chieftainess of Monango. You and white woman will come before her. You stole great jewel of Akada and Mea angry. Very angry. We search for you many moons and now find you. Come!'

Anjani hesitated, about to say that he had had nothing to do with the theft of the jewel of Akada, then as he realised how hopeless it would be to argue with so many warriors around him, he held his counsel. Perhaps he could explain things a little more easily to the mysterious Mea.

'What does he say?' Rita asked anxiously. 'Are we captives or something?'

'Afraid so,' Anjani answered grimly. 'We've come to a part of the jungle I've never encountered before. Seems there's a high chieftainess or something who has the impression I stole the jewel of Akada. We've to come before her.'

Rita looked dismayed, and even more so when Anjani had given her the full story, but by this time both of them were on their way down the valley slope with the natives on either side of them.

The journey took the party across the valley floor, then up a long, rugged acclivity in the cliff face, and so finally to its summit. Here there was a region of towering rock, blazing hot in the sunshine, which presently gave way to jungle again. A long slope appeared and in the base of it there stood a city, every bit as strange as Akada itself, though less corroded with time and weather, and every bit as beautiful. There were temples, orderly palm-lined streets, terraces gay with tropical flowers, colonnades up which twining plants were coiled in lividly bright festoons.

'Monango!' the black chief said, pointing. 'Monango where Terrible Highness, Mea, rule. You go there.'

'If Mea is as artistic as the city she rules I don't think we have much to fear,' Rita commented, clinging to Anjani's massive arm as they went forward again. 'And you mean to say you never knew such a place existed?'

'I hadn't the least idea. As a rule I stay only where the jungle is, which means I never came this far.'

Before long the main street of the city had been reached. On either side of it white stone dwellings stood, some tall some only with one story, and none with any windows. Yet each had a definitely delicate architecture and bespoke the skill of craftsmen probably long gone. The most surprising thing was the amount of gold everywhere. It was on every dome and roof, and one building even had gold steps. In fact, the precious metal seemed to be cheap as stone itself.

The black leader finally turned into one of the buildings in the centre of the street, an edifice with enormous metal doors — wide open — made all the more impressive by gold studs driven into it. He led the way along a cool, polished stone hall, with mosaic-patterned floor, and eventually into a long low room where half lowered raffia blinds shut out the blaze of the tropical sun.

There seemed to be any number of skin rugs and costly tapestries on the walls, and a great deal of furniture carved out of solid ivory. Upon a distant couch sprawled amidst silk cushions, with two ebon-skinned men waving a fan gently above her, lay a woman. She raised herself slightly on her elbow as the leader of the guards spoke. As before he used the queer tongue that Anjani was just able to understand.

'I bring you the thief of Akada, Terrible One.' He bowed low. 'Together with the white woman.'

Mea, for presumably it was she, motioned with her hand. Immediately every man in the room made a bowing and servile exit. Anjani and Rita were left a few feet away from the high chieftainess, studying her intently.

She was more striking than actually beautiful, olive-skinned and green-eyed. Her thick black hair fell to her smooth, uncovered shoulders, and was as dark as midnight. Her form, almost nakedly visible, was roped about with great coils of pearls and glittering jewels and Rita at least found herself gazing with fascinated interest at the enormous rubies which crowned the apex of the woman's breast-plates.

'You are . . . Mea?' Anjani questioned at length, using the tribal tongue.

The woman smiled, and it had much of a tigress in it. Her teeth were small and white, but there was a way in which her upper lip drew back which was incarnate cruelty.

'You have no need, white one, to use the tribal tongue when addressing me,' she responded, her voice gentle and yet mocking. 'I am an intelligent woman, the last of a highly intelligent race who understood every major language in the world. Sit down, both of you.'

The order came in a sudden whip-crack of authority and the olive-arm motioned from amidst the ropes of jewels. They fell aside from it with a faint, intriguing rattle.

Rita and Anjani did as they were told, glanced at each other, then back to the woman. She stirred lazily on the silken cushions, every movement of her rounded limbs as graceful as those of a cat.

'Yes, I am Mea, high Chieftainess of Monango,' she assented at length. 'I brought you here, white one, because you stole the sacred jewel of Akada — the flame-stone, which has been the possession of my race for untold centuries.'

'I did not steal it,' Anjani answered

quietly. 'It was my brother, an identical twin to myself.'

'You tell lies easily, white one! Around Akada there are always guardians of my race, unseen but watchful. They saw you and this white woman, and that is enough.'

'Possibly they did, because we were also in Akada, trapped there by my brother. If they saw this woman and me, then they should also have seen him.'

'They saw you, and this story of an identical brother I do not believe!'

Anjani was silent, realising that his twin had been mistaken for himself in every instance, and plainly the woman was not eager to listen to the truth.

'At first my fury was greater than the tempest,' Mea resumed presently. 'I have lain here and planned the most vicious tortures for your daring to steal the Akada jewel — but now you are before me I have forgotten everything I ever planned.' Mea was silent, her green eyes ranging over Anjani's mighty form. 'You are massive, white man,' she reflected.

Anjani half rose, on the verge of

argument, then he sat down again slowly. He had just noticed that to the rear of the couch on which Mea was lying there lay two black panthers. Their heads were cocked now, their green eyes fixed on Anjani. Evidently they were guarding Mea. Anjani half-smiled to himself. He could easily have dealt with the panthers if necessity had demanded it, but at the moment he was anxious to learn more.

'You are well protected, Chieftainess,' he commented.

Mea glanced over her shoulder and nodded musingly. 'I call them Night and Day, because you cannot have one without the other. They were born of panthers who originated in Java, and I would not advise you to anger them . . . or me.'

'Look,' Rita said, abruptly, her own summing-up of the woman at an end, 'is this supposed to be a social call, a pleasant chit-chat, or what? What do you want with us?'

'With you, white woman, nothing. To me you rank only as dust — But with you, white man, it is different.'

Anjani eyed her and waited.

'I no longer resent your stealing the Akada jewel,' Mea continued. 'You can be of immense value to me. Such a man as you at the head of my new race could not be bettered.'

'I don't understand,' Anjani replied, shrugging.

'I said I was the last of my race, and I meant it. I am a woman, and what use is a woman alone without a man when the rest of the race is dead? I see no reason why such a magnificent creature as you cannot become the High Chieftain.'

'Marry you, you mean?' Rita gasped, astonished.

'Men and women have married before, white woman,' Mea commented dryly, 'but to few women has there been granted such a man as *this*!'

'You can forget all about that this moment,' Anjani said. 'The only woman I intend to marry is seated beside me.'

Mea laughed, and that feline quality in it became more pronounced than ever. For some reason Rita felt afraid, knowing how pitiless her own sex might prove.

'You have forgotten,' Mea said, 'that you cannot leave this city, white man. Strong though you are, mighty though your muscles may be, you are the absolute slave of my will. I have decided you shall be the High Chieftain of Monango, and nothing you might do can stop it!'

The ring of authority was back in the voice. Anjani sprang to his feet in fury and the two panthers scrambled up too and stood snarling, waiting, held back by chains of solid gold to their jewel-studded collars.

'Lie down!' Mea spat at them, and they obeyed; then she uncoiled herself from the couch and stood up. She was a woman of superb figure and carriage now she could be seen in an erect pose. She stood perhaps five feet nine and every curve and line was symmetry itself. Anjani remained standing, watching her narrowly.

'There is much you do not know about my race, white man,' Mea said coldly. 'We were once the proudest, mightiest race in all the world. Then misfortune and disease came upon us and our greatness dwindled until we had only the Africa continent. Our numbers were not great enough to permit of us challenging the evergrowing millions of the outer world, so we came into the jungle and built our cities. Four of them — Monango, which is the chief city, and three others — Beltanzi, Viljo, and Akada. They all exist in the forest but apparently, so far, you have only discovered Akada. Akada, like the other two cities, is used as a storehouse for our treasures — and you *dared* steal our racial jewel!'

'I tell you again, I did *not*!' Anjani retorted.

'You are a fool, white man! Would you have me believe that there can be two such men as you abroad in Africa?'

'There are, whether you believe it or not — though I can well understand your slaves getting mixed up and, seeing two men identical, take them to be one, myself.'

'Whatever the answer, you are here,' Mea said deliberately. 'There are no men left in my race — or women either — and for years I have struggled to think how my race might still be made to continue until it can again achieve its former magnificence and wealth. You are the answer.'

'As I told you before, I refuse.'

'Refuse? You cannot! You have no choice!'

Anjani clenched his fists and shot a glance at Rita. She was looking at Mea in profound disgust, but not a little fear.

'And the white woman?' Anjani asked. 'You do not even mention her in your plans.'

'I have no reason to. I have no use for a white woman who is not of my race and who obviously hates me. You are betrothed to her, white man, therefore that source of competition must be removed.'

'What!' Rita jumped up in fury. 'Are you daring to say, Chieftainess, that you'll — you'll kill me?'

Mea shrugged, her green eyes pitiless. 'One usually kills that which is useless, white woman.'

'But — '

'You're not killing her and you're not

having me,' Anjani stated flatly. 'Call all the guards you like, turn loose all the panthers in the palace, and we'll still get away, starting now. Come on, Rita!'

He grabbed her arm and hurried her across the mosaic floor. Instantly Mea swung and uncoupled the gold chains holding the panthers. With eager snarls they hurtled forward, one knocking Rita flying helplessly across the polished floor and the other one arriving as Anjani swung round.

He was just in time to prevent the outspread claws from striking down his face. Instantly his mighty hands closed on the black, muscular throat and he bore the panther to the floor, using all his jungle knowledge to keep clear of the deadly, ripping claws. Never once releasing his steel grip he battered the magnificent head of the beast hard upon the floor until the constant impacts partly stunned its senses.

Only then did he whip one hand free and snatch out his knife. The blade flashed once, straight to the beast's heart. It relaxed, quivering, glossy coat rippling with a final reaction.

Rita, for her part, was lying flat on her back, her arms outflung, completely unable to move. Standing astride her with its snarling lips only six inches from her face was the remaining panther, evidently trained not to bite unless so ordered. Mea, in the background, folded her shapely arms and laughed outright.

'The white woman does not seem particularly at ease,' she commented dryly.

Anjani flashed the cynical chieftainess a look, then he put his knife between his teeth and crept in on the panther from the rear. It became suddenly aware of the impending attack and jumped round in cat-like agility, flattening for a spring. Anjani leapt to one side as the spring came and at the same moment snatched his knife from his teeth and drove it right into the beast's neck. It screamed with the pain and crashed onto the floor. Still very much alive, however, and trailing blood down its coat, it leapt again, Anjani crouching.

Dropping his knife he clutched the

broad throat with one hand and a back leg with the other, then with every ounce of his stupendous strength he hurled the black body against the nearest wall. Under the tremendous impact bones crunched and broke against each other and the already wounded beast flattened out, not yet dead but injured sufficiently to prevent its being of further danger.

Anjani whipped up his knife, swept Rita up under one arm, then hurtled for the door. Mea's expression had changed completely and anger had given her olive cheeks a rosy flush. She screamed out some kind of order and the door flew open, revealing two black guards with spears levelled.

Anjani put Rita down on her feet then charged straight at the two men, ducking under their uncertainly waving spears. His right fist slammed under the jaw of the man nearest and knocked him spinning into the corridor. The other man he lifted by throat and loincloth, high over his head, and flung on top of his struggling comrade — then he was out in the corridor, Rita keeping beside him.

Three more guards came hurrying forward. Anjani stopped, measuring them. To the rear Mea had appeared and was screaming orders. The guards levelled their spears.

Anjani glanced behind him, then suddenly swung and raced over to Mea. She was so astonished at his hurtling rush she just gaped at him. His intention, however, to use her as a shield for himself, was scotched as one of the guards made a random throw with his spear. The point missed its mark but the heavy ivory shaft struck Anjani a terrific crack on the side of the head. Half stunned and his head exploding with stars he dropped on his knees. The next thing he knew he was seized, his massive arms held tightly whilst chain was being wound about his ankles.

'You are stronger than I ever imagined, white man,' Mea murmured, her green eyes full of brief feminine admiration. 'What a chief you will make for Monango!'

Anjani tightened his lips. His head was

clearing and he strove with all his huge strength to break free, but without any effect. The guards knew what they were tackling and held on tenaciously.

'Take the woman away,' Mea snapped. 'She will make an interesting exhibit at the marriage festivities.'

One of the guards released his hold on Anjani and caught at Rita's arm, holding her tightly. She certainly had not the strength to deal with the native and could only give Anjani a dumb, helpless look — then she was dragged away down the corridor, protesting and shouting as she went. Anjani turned his head at last and eyed Mea.

'What did you mean by her making an interesting exhibit?' he demanded. 'I warn you, Mea, if anything happens to her I will bring this whole city of Monango down round your ears! I'll do more: I'll kill you too! It will be the worst day's work you ever did if you try and marry me and harm the white woman.'

'I have an objective and I shall achieve it,' Mea snapped back, her green eyes glinting, 'The woman shall become food

79

for the Sacred Ones at the festivities. It is many a moon since they tasted the delicate flesh of the female. They will be appeased indeed. The woman, I fancy, will make a tasty morsel. Tonight, white man, we shall dine in comfort: tomorrow we shall be wed, and at my command you shall watch the festivities as punishment for your destroying my beloved Night and Day. You are strong, white man, but, oh, so foolish!'

Anjani struggled again, but still to no purpose,

'It will be better that you are fed by force,' Mea mused. 'To once free you would enable you to carry out your promise to bring Monango down round my ears, and that is a chance I do not wish to take . . . Feed him,' she broke off, 'and then bring him back to me.'

* * *

'Something,' Crespin said, 'has got to be done, boys.'

The first mate, together with his comrades, was sprawled at the far side of

80

a clearing from Tocoto and his blacks where a halt had been called for the night. In the clearing centre a fire was crackling, kept fed by one of the natives. Otherwise there was comparative peace except for the usual night cries from the wilderness.

'But what?' one of the crew growled, feeling uncomfortable after a meal which had been mostly fruit. 'We know this is Tocoto, but what are we going to do about it? He's got all the natives on his side, and will continue to have as long as that jewel remains in that bag round his neck. The natives are obviously scared to death.'

'We must get the jewel,' Crespin mused, wiping sweat from his forehead with his sleeve.

'How?' asked another. 'Go up to him and say, 'Would you mind, Tocoto'? I don't think there's anything we can do.'

'There's got to be,' Crespin insisted. 'We've got to stop him getting to Akada for one thing, and for another we must try and find Mrs. Perrivale, and Anjani, of course. There is only one way to do that

81

and that is with the help of these natives whom Tocoto has under his control. If we get hold of the jewel we give the orders.'

'You still think Mrs. Perrivale is alive then? I doubt it, just as I doubt if Anjani is either.'

'Just the same we must try every possible line, and the next best one is to get these natives on our side. If Tocoto once gets to Akada he'll move all the treasure out and everything we've sweated and toiled for will have been useless. Even without Mrs. Perrivale, if we fail to find her, we have the authority to remove the treasure: she fixed all that up with Captain Hart and the lawyers back home.'

The men were silent for a while, looking towards Tocoto's distant form. Being white, he was fairly visible, lounging with his back against a tree, resting after the hard march that had been made during the daytime.

'When he sleeps,' Crespin murmured, 'I'll risk it.'

'Unarmed?' demanded the man next to him. 'Don't do it, chief. It'd be suicide!

He's stronger than a gorilla and if he catches you — '

'I know the danger. I'm going to risk it just the same.'

And Crespin meant exactly what he said. He relaxed in an attitude of sleep, but made no effort to doze off. Instead he kept himself alert, long after the men around him had nodded into slumber. It seemed an interminable time to Crespin before the blacks and the giant white man were genuinely asleep, and even then he had the solitary native doing fire duty to worry about.

Silent, immovable, Crespin weighed up the chances. The native watching the fire was not armed, and his spear was some distance off with those of his fellows. At the moment he squatted on his haunches, staring into the flames, a pile of brushwood beside him. Crespin's gaze strayed from him to the only weapon he could see — a fair-sized heavy stone lying within reach in the undergrowth. He stirred lazily in his apparent sleep, grabbed the stone, then lay for a long time motionless until at last he observed that the eyes of the solitary black had moved from him again.

The next move depended entirely on how accurate Crespin could make his aim. In his day he had been a champion cricketer and a demon bowler, so if the flair still remained he might succeed in delivering one smashing blow to that woolly head which would give him the chance he wanted.

He had no sooner made up his mind to strike than he acted. Sitting up suddenly he measured the distance, then hurled the stone with every ounce of his strength. The native did not see it coming though he was trying to fathom Crespin's movements. Then the savage blow he received on the centre of the forehead keeled him over backwards on his heels and he ceased to take any more interest in the proceedings.

At the sounds Tocoto stirred for a moment, stretched his powerful arms, then curled down again to sleep. Crespin waited, sweat trickling down his face. Ultimately he felt it was safe to risk it and slowly got on his feet. He had to move before the stunned black recovered and gave the alarm.

As silently as he could, half crouched, moving step by step, Crespin advanced towards the sleeping jungle man. When he was a yard away from him he stopped and looked at the bag lying on the massive chest. Then his gaze dropped to the knife in Tocoto's loincloth. Would it be possible to whip out that knife, slash the thong of the jewel-bag, and jump free all in one movement? No. Crespin very much doubted it. There was only one alternative: kill Tocoto.

From this Crespin shrank, not because he had any love for Tocoto but because he was, by nature, a man of quiet temperament and the thought of deliberately slaying a man, even if he was half wild, when he was sleeping was repugnant to him. Yet if he did not . . . ?

He *had* to. There was no other way out, and personal sentiment just did not enter into it. So he began moving towards the nearest native who, spear beside him, was fast asleep. Very gently Crespin picked it up and then turned. The instant he did so he froze in his tracks —

Tocoto was standing up, his mighty fists clenched and his eyes fixed on Crespin in the firelight. Evidently he had heard everything and been perfectly aware of what was going on. Crespin hesitated — then with a final effort he raised the spear over his head preparatory to flinging it.

But he did not succeed. Tocoto pounced, seized the hapless first mate by the throat and bore him to the ground. Crespin shouted and gurgled helplessly and the sound aroused the entire camp, whites and blacks alike. Immediately Crespin's comrades were on their feet, dashing to his aid but they were held back by the menacing points of spears.

All they could do was watch the death of Crespin as his struggles became weaker and the relentless fingers of Tocoto never relaxed for a moment. When at last all signs of struggle had ceased he picked up the motionless body, raised it over his head, then flung it away into the undergrowth. He spoke in the tribal tongue and, though not as familiar with it as Crespin had been, the remaining white men did understand the gist of it.

'For that you shall all of you suffer. I will spare you no mercy henceforth on the march to Akada. No man, least of all a man who is not of the jungle, can attack Tocoto the Mighty and expect to live. Let the fate of your comrade be a lesson to you!'

4

In the arena

Dawn shafted its light over the fabulous city of Monango. The rays of the rising sun struck Anjani as he lay on a comfortable bed, his feet chained to it and his wrists so shackled that, whilst he still had movement, he could not get free. He stirred slowly from an uneasy slumber. It had been haunted by thoughts of what had happened to Rita, of whom he had not heard or seen anything since she had been taken away by the guard in the main entrance hall.

With a clinking of chain Anjani sat up. The four guards watching him became more alert. One of them signalled and the next thing Anjani knew he was being released. He tried to break free but even his giant muscles could not cope with four exceptionally powerful men armed with spears, so he submitted to being taken into an enormous and elaborate room next his own where he was ordered to bathe in the immense stone-lined pool.

He did so without murmur but was not allowed a knife with which to shave — in case he used it for other purposes. When his ablutions were over rich garments were held out to him but he shook his head.

'Anjani never wear clothes. Skin not able to bear it.'

The clothes were offered with more insistence, but he still shook his head and tightened the thong about his regirdled loincloth instead. The natives looked at one another, then one of them departed, presumably to discover from the High Chieftainess what should be done. When the man returned he said briefly:

'Her Terrible Highness permit you to stay unclad, but you in wrong clothes for ceremony of betrothal. Her Terrible Highness is angry as the tempest.'

'So am I,' Anjani retorted. 'And there is not going to be a betrothal, either!'

The guards did not comment on this assertion. Instead Anjani was motioned back into his room and forced to have a breakfast of fruits, curious tasting bread, and light wine. Then, watched relentlessly on every side he was led down the main corridor outside and finally into the great room that seemed to be Mea's own quarters.

Anjani, much though he hated the woman, was yet man enough to be impressed by her extraordinary fascination on this morning. Though she did not possess beauty in the accepted sense she had none the less a subtle, fatal attraction about her which Anjani found it difficult to ignore. She had discarded the ropes of pearls and jewels which had barely served to conceal her the previous evening and was now attired in a flowing creation of flame colour, the skirt a mass of billowing folds and the bodice sleeveless and extremely low cut. The only ornament was a gigantic diamond in the exact centre of the waistline, which seemed to hold the entire *ensemble* together.

'Good morning, white man,' she murmured, slanting her green eyes towards Anjani as he was brought in. 'I was angered when you would not wear the betrothal costume, as I am doing, but with you I cannot be angry for long.'

She came forward as she spoke, radiating a heavy, seductive perfume. Anjani said nothing as her soft arms went about his powerful neck.

'Why do you not bow to the inevitable, white man?' she murmured softly. 'Can I not give you so much more than that other white creature with whom you came here? You can have not only me, but all the wealth of the race. And you shall, because I will not be turned aside.'

Anjani took her arms firmly in his hands and forced them down to her sides.

'Go through with this, Mea, and you'll regret it to the end of your days. I have already warned you of that.'

She smiled. 'Why do you hate me so? So magnificent in everything except mood. Am I so terrible? So utterly unlike what a woman should be?'

'That's nothing to with it. You think only of yourself and the enforcement of your wishes. Where is the white woman?'

The bare shoulders, satin-smooth, rose

and fell negatively.

'We shall see her presently — when the festivities begin. For the moment only the betrothal matters.'

Anjani hesitated over some kind of desperate move, but he was not allowed to make it for at a signal from their Chieftainess the guards came forward and once again. Anjani was powerless to break free. He was turned about, led from the great room, down the hall, and then to the outdoors. For a while there was a march along the blazingly hot street which ended at an ornamental affair like a gigantic sedan. Into this, amidst silken cushions, Anjani was thrust. Before very long Mea appeared, followed by black servants holding feather fans above her to keep away the saturating sunlight. She settled next to Anjani as he sat with folded arms, his face grim.

'You are not a smiling bridegroom, white man,' Mea reminded him. 'If you are thinking of ways to escape you are thinking idly. Surrounded by my retinue you stand no chance whatever.'

Anjani did not answer. The sedan was

raised on the massive shoulders of the blacks and the ceremonial cortege started off down the street.

The journey ended at a tremendous amphitheatre which — had Anjani been versed in civilised history — would have reminded him of the days of Imperial Rome. On all sides of the huge arena were the tiers of seats, made of stone, and argent-white in the sunshine. Beyond, mysterious and deeply green, loomed the eternal jungle.

Nor were the seats of the amphitheatre empty. Blacks filled them on every hand, blacks who rose in obedience as Mea's ceremonial sedan appeared. With perfect majesty she stepped forth into the sunlight and walked with dignity to the two seats at the amphitheatre's highest point. Anjani was forced to follow her and sat down beside her. Then the blacks reseated themselves and there came the sound of weird, dirging music.

'How long does the betrothal take, and who performs it?' Anjani asked at last.

Mea laughed gently. 'It is pleasant to know that the white man will still speak to me,' she murmured. 'As to our betrothal, it is already performed. You are mine, and I am yours.'

'What?' Anjani looked at her in bewilderment, knowing that even the wildest tribes had a more tangible marriage ceremony than this.

'The ceremony is dictated by circumstances,' Mea explained, with a little sigh. 'Since I am the only surviving member of my race there are none of the elders left to pronounce the union — so, before the last elder died, it was agreed that the act of sitting in the ruling seats of the race — where we are now — would be considered also the act of union and marriage. You, white man, are now the recognised High Chieftain of Monango and all that it entails.'

Anjani did not speak for a moment. He was listening half detachedly to the strange music played by invisible 'musicians' somewhere in the amphitheatre, and on the other hand he was even feeling sorry for this fantastic, lonely woman who was ready to sacrifice everything so that her race might still rise again.

Then Anjani forgot his speculations and looked up sharply over the heads of the blacks in the immediate seats below. Things were happening in the arena — but they did not interest him particularly. To the accompaniment of the music the party of magnificently muscled blacks who had appeared began a series of gymnastic feats to prove their physical prowess. It set Anjani wondering where all these black men had come from since they did not fall into any tribal category he could place. Finally he assumed that they were descendants of servants who had always been connected with Mea's people.

The gymnastics over, dancing followed and the music grew more wild. Anjani watched in boredom, thinking of Rita and wondering where she was. It was about this time that the question was answered for him as Rita was brought into the arena, a tiny figure in her torn white clothes, her hands bound tightly behind her, hair flowing, and a giant black on either side of her.

Anjani stiffened and sat erect. He

glanced about him sharply and was aware of two blacks to his rear with their spears at such an angle they could use them instantly. Then he met Mea's cruel green eyes.

'I hope this will awaken you from your lethargy, white man,' she murmured. 'If it should awaken you too much, remember that you are watched on every side.'

Anjani switched his gaze back to the arena. The helpless Rita was standing motionless now in the arena's approximate centre, a long length of chain leading from a band about her waist — which at this distance looked like silver — to a stake driven deep in the ground. Her hands were released and then she stood looking fearfully around her in the brilliant sunlight as the blacks made haste to depart. Finally, except for the solitary, frightened girl the arena was empty.

The colour began to rise in the back of Anjani's thick neck and his lips tightened. Mea stole a sly glance at him and then looked back towards Rita. At that moment a massive, tawny beast appeared from the far end of the arena, released through a trap. Two others followed it. The tawny aspect was created by the shadows of the walls for when the massive creatures padded into the full sunlight they became revealed as striped. There were cries of delight from the assembled blacks in the tiers of seats and Mea strained forward a little in her seat to watch in sadistic glee.

'The Sacred Ones,' she explained, giving Anjani a quick glance. 'Are they not beautiful? Many, many years ago they were brought from one of the cities my ancestors ruled, a city on the far side of the world. Magnificent, are they not?'

Anjani did not answer. He had never seen anything like the animals before — which was not to be wondered at. They were, in truth, sabre-toothed tigers, the mighty and ferocious progenitors of the modern Asiatic tiger, creatures which had roamed the earth in long-gone ages and which, in this case, had evidently been preserved and bred by the unholy ancestors of the High Chieftainess.

Rita gave a scream of terror and started running, forgetting the chain. It suddenly brought her up short and she crashed helplessly on her face in the dust. She twisted her head and watched the still distant animals as they sniffed the ground, then the air, and finally stood looking at her.

Anjani felt his scalp crawling. He had never seen such fangs on any animals before — two gigantic fighting fangs in the top jaw, so long they were almost small tusks. Then the great heads, magnificently marked, and the blazing green of the eyes. Anjani shifted helplessly as Mea gave a little gurgle of laughter and clapped her hands in delight.

Anjani clenched his fingers against the stone armrests of his chair, and one of the rests gave way. The stone, weather-beaten and old, had cracked under the unaccustomed pressure. Anjani's eyes narrowed as he looked down at the chunk of stone left in his hand. Mea had not noticed; neither had the blacks. They were too intent on Rita as she reeled about like a goat on a cord trying to escape the relentless investigation of the deadly beasts.

The first one, evidently the hungriest, reached a spot a few yards away and stood with nostrils twitching. Mea threw back her head and laughed outright.

'They are so slow!' she exclaimed, in the tone of one who humours tiresome children. 'It is such a long time since there was a sacrifice they hardly know what to do — but soon they will strike — '

Anjani did not waste a second longer: he did not dare if Rita were to be saved. He suddenly leapt to his feet, stone in his hand, and smashed it down with terrific force against the heart of the black nearest him. His chest stove in and bleeding the man toppled helplessly forward, straight into the jungle man's arms. Instantly Ajani whipped him from his feet and flung him onto the down-thrusting spear from the second guardian black.

It was only a momentary advantage since all the blacks were instantly ready for action, but Anjani had taken this into full consideration. He caught the aston-ished Mea beneath the arms, whirled her up from her seat, and held her in front of him. It was the trick he had tried to pull back in the palace hall, and failed: perhaps this time it would prove more effective.

Mea kicked and struggled savagely, but he took no notice. He began backing down the steps between the tiers, keeping the blacks with raised spears at bay for fear they struck their Chieftainess. She screamed and struggled wildly but to dislodge the grip Anjani had of her was impossible. She was the perfect screen, and he meant using her.

In a few moments he had gained the lofty, encircling stone wall which completely ringed the arena. Changing his hold on Mea so that she was swept into his arms he held her tightly as he jumped the fifteen feet down to the arena itself. At the end of the jump he stumbled, Mea tumbling out of his grip. Instantly she flew at him in hysterical fury, but with one brush of his mighty arm he sent her stumbling away from him and raced across to where the nearest sabre-tooth was investigating a couple of yards from the paralysed Rita.

Desperate hope came into her eyes as she saw Anjani speeding towards her. Reaching her, he swung her behind him. The tiger snarled, and flattened its belly to the earth. To the rear the remaining two tigers came padding up. Anjani gave a desperate look around him and at that same moment a spear landed near him from one of the warriors crowded on the encircling wall.

Though the spear had been intended to impale him, it was also a perfect weapon. Anjani whipped it up and gave it to the girl. The sabre-tooth, still wondering about its prey, was watching the spear now, just as a cat might suddenly become interested in something unexpected. Anjani took the chance to seize Rita's chain, bending the links slowly in his powerful fingers.

Meanwhile, Mea was screaming for help and trying vainly to scale the lofty wall. The blacks did not attempt to give her any assistance, so apparently they preferred her to be in difficulties — but they did continue to throw spears at

Anjani in the hope of hitting him. Practically all of them fell short, however, because of his distance away.

Then suddenly the tiger sprang, to the accompaniment of a soul-chilling scream. But Anjani had seen the spring coming. He yanked the spear from Rita and drove it with savage force straight into the beast, the shaft burying itself between the blazing eyes. The monster seemed to turn over in the air and crash into the dust, stone dead, its brain shattered . . . Then came the other two sabre-tooths, much more warily, perhaps warned by the fate of their comrade.

The second one lunged suddenly, straight for Rita. Anjani intercepted it, and the heavy body crashed him over onto the ground. Up came his hands, buried in the glossy coat, his iron muscles fighting to keep the terrible fangs away from his face and throat. Slowly he edged his knees under the beast's belly, then with a supreme effort of arms and legs hurled the creature away from him and sprang up.

Diving, he snatched up one of the

many spears that had been flung at him, and drove it hard into the tiger's breast as he leapt again. It stopped in its tracks, not killing it, but preventing it having free movement because the spear was right through its massive body, the hand-end pressing on the ground.

Anjani breathed hard and looked around him. The last of the sabre-tooths was eyeing him, ears down, belly on the ground, black murder in his flaming green eyes. It sprang, with a blood-curdling shriek. Anjani sprang, too, using one of his old jungle tricks. The leap took him high over the creature and he landed backwards on the broad back. Instantly he twisted around, his forearms locked under the creature's slavering jowls. He began to exert the maximum backward pressure of which he was capable, forcing the tiger's head upward and at the same time maintaining a crushing knee grip on the spine.

Mea, evidently realising she was in danger of losing her one chance of a husband, snatched up a fallen spear and held it over her head, looking for an opportunity to plunge it into the tiger . . .

The creature's roars of pain and fury made the ground quake and his front paws lashed helplessly in the air as his head was lifted. Sweating, his face a mask of strain, Anjani dragged further and further backwards with unrelenting power, the muscles and tendons of his arms and shoulders leaping into corded knots with the effort.

Rita, motionless and fascinated, watched the struggle — then she gave a gasp of horror as she saw the tiger with the shaft through it crawling on its belly towards Mea as she pranced around with her spear. Too late she saw the dying but still ferocious tiger almost upon her: she was also too late to dodge the terrific blow it struck her with its front paw. Lacerated and crying aloud in pain she staggered a few feet and then collapsed in the dust, blood smearing her face and shoulders.

Rita turned her head away. The tiger dragged on again, its jaws snarling, and there was the sound of crushing bone, and Mea's anguished screaming . . . Anjani was aware in a remote kind of way of what was taking place, but he had quite enough troubles of his own. His strength, gigantic though it was, was proving unequal to the task of completely snapping the great beast's neck, and the more he failed in achieving his objective the more the last sabre-tooth, knew it and fought to recover the ascendancy.

Rita, for her part, steeled herself to the ghastly sight of Mea being torn to pieces by the furious, mortally wounded animal. At least it had saved her from death, and she might yet be able to spare Mea from further horror. She crept to the limit of her chain, reached a spear, and then held it over her head. With what strength she possessed she drove it into the tiger over the left shoulder — which, as she remembered, ought to be a vital spot. Evidently it was for the beast quivered in the midst of its activities and then, overcome by this final outrage upon it, it flattened in the dust and quivered.

Rita jerked her gaze away. Mea could not be saved. Nothing *could* save that. Above, on the wall, the blacks were

chanting and moaning amongst themselves, presumably at the death of their
Chieftainess.

At this same moment Anjani had to
release his hold on the sabre-tooth. He
did so and sprang free to avoid being
torn to pieces. He dived instantly for the
spear that Rita had flung into the now
almost dead tiger and pulled it free. Just
in time he flung it into the mouth of the
remaining tiger as it flew at him.

Viciously the creature bit downwards in
an effort to snap the shaft but the solid
ivory was too much even for those huge
central fangs — so for the next few
moments the tiger was preoccupied with
tearing helplessly at his face with his
claws, looking like a monstrous dog trying
to dislodge a fishbone.

Anjani took immediate advantage of
the situation and sprang again to the
chain holding Rita. With savage energy he
resumed his straining and twisting at the
link he had started to break. Back and
forth he bent it in his powerful fingers
until finally it broke and Rita was free,
except for the short length fastened to the

silver band around her waist. This Anjani did not bother about. Catching the girl's arm he turned to run with her to the far end of the arena. In that direction the blacks were non-existent, all of them having congregated at this nearer point to watch the hair-raising proceedings below.

The remaining sabre-tooth, however, had other ideas. By driving his head into the ground he succeeded in dislodging the spear thrust into his jaws, even though he must have severely lacerated the inside of his throat in the process. Anjani and Rita had not progressed more than a dozen feet before the creature came bounding after them.

'Quickly!' Anjani gasped, and flung Rita in one direction whilst he vaulted in the other. The tiger blundered between them, his speed preventing him calculating exactly. Wheeling, Anjani raced back to the spear the beast had dislodged.

He whipped it up, started running — and kept on running, even when the sabre-tooth flattened for the spring. Just as it rose into the air Anjani flung the spear with all his power straight into the breast where lay the savage heart. It was a dead true aim. The tiger reared in anguish for a moment, screamed deafeningly, and then slumped down on crumbling legs. Finally it dropped on its side and became still.

Anjani breathed hard and drew the back of his hand over his sweat-dewed face. He dragged the spear from the dead beast and caught hold of Rita again.

'We've got to get out of here somehow,' he told her, looking about him. 'And these blacks are not going to make it any easier. Our only chance is to outrun them to the other end of the arena and escape into the jungle — They'll be hindered in any case by the tiers of seats blocking the way . . . Come — quickly!'

Anjani was running hard even as he spoke, Rita stumbling along beside him. Finally he threw her over his shoulder; and gained considerable impetus thereby. A glance satisfied him that the blacks, too, were moving, but just as he had expected they were being slowed down by the seats barring their way.

Anjani reached the further wall of the

arena well ahead of them, making for the trap through which the tigers had been released. This gave him the chance of a step-up to the wall top — and he took it in a flying leap, hurling the spear up ahead of him.

With a tremendous effort, Rita's weight encumbering him somewhat, he hauled himself up to the top of the trap, then jumped again, his fingers gripping the wall top. In a matter of a few seconds he was over, the distant blacks hurling spears and screaming with fury at being delayed in getting at him.

The delay was absolute as far as they were concerned. Anjani now had open landscape and the jungle beyond it, so with spear in hand and Rita now racing beside him he ran harder than he had ever done in his life, until the wilderness closed around him and the girl. Once this happened he found a tree, climbed it, and settled Rita on a massive, jutting branch. Surrounded by the screen of leaves all danger of being detected had gone — which was just as well for, before very long, there came the sound of the black warriors searching the undergrowth and shouting to one another in their native tongue.

Anjani grinned as he watched them then he turned to the shaken, slowly recovering girl.

'I do not think we shall ever be nearer to disaster than we were back in the arena,' he commented. 'You are not hurt, little one?'

'No — thanks to you, but I could breathe better if this band could be taken from my waist.'

Anjani nodded, examined it, then after a while discovered the secret of the clamp that sealed it. He pulled out the pin and the silver band fell away. Reaching out, he hung it on a small tree branch.

'You saw what happened to Mea?' Rita questioned, rubbing her waistline tenderly. 'It was ghastly!'

'Yes. Torn to pieces by one of the sacred ones! Well, I am afraid Mea was a very savage and lonely woman. Maybe she will be happier dead.'

'It also means the last member of her race died when she went,' Rita said. 'That leaves the four cities she spoke of as open treasure, for anybody who wishes — us, I hope — to take away. The greatest trouble will be the black slaves who obeyed her. I cannot understand why they should want to pursue us. Surely they ought to be happier with Mea out of the way? She can't have given them an easy time of it.'

'We don't know what threat she held over them,' Anjani replied, thinking. 'She may even have told them that if anything happened to her she would be watching them, even after death, so rather than incur her wrath the blacks are still on the lookout or those she hated and wanted — you and myself respectively. And don't forget the jewel that Tocoto has. That, I think, is the real reason why the blacks are searching. They believe I took it, and they also believe the jewel gives them a kind of dominion. I doubt if we shall ever be safe from them.'

'What, then, is our next move?'

'There can only be one, to find Tocoto. If I can do that, destroy him, and recover the jewel of Akada I will see that these blacks get it back since it is their racial property — or at any rate the property of the race that they formerly served. But Tocoto I must find. Until he is out of the way I shall never feel that I can leave the jungle . . . '

5

Devil mud!

In a matter of four more days Tocoto and his army of natives, with the thirst-weary white men working harder than anybody — exactly as Tocoto had promised they should — Akada was in sight. The jungle had been left behind and the final march across the blistering desert remained, Akada itself looming in the distance with the shimmering uncertainty of a mirage.

Tocoto's plans were all laid. Once Akada was reached he was resolved upon removing all the treasures it contained and having them transported by his native followers back into the jungle. In fact his hopes were high and he was thoroughly enjoying his role as a swaggering overlord, given complete mastery over otherwise rebellious natives by the jewel that he carried at his neck.

The smattering of white men were

quite beyond comment. On the journey through the jungle they had been compelled to do most of the hacking and cutting of the interminable vegetation, and every time they had flagged at all in their efforts a whip wielded by one of the natives had flayed across their naked shoulders. Food and water they had been given in very sparing amounts, hardly enough to keep them moving, yet sufficient to save them from dying. Tocoto enjoyed every minute of it, taking full revenge for the attack first mate Crespin had attempted to make upon him.

It was evening and a refreshing coolness was coming when Akada lay only half a mile away, silent, mysterious. And apparently deserted. With no thought of possible dangers Tocoto continued advancing. He only realised the consequences of his lack of caution when, the city finally being reached, there suddenly came a hail of spears and poison-tipped arrows from amongst the roofs of the buildings.

The effect on the natives around Tocoto was devastating. Never expecting an onslaught half a dozen of them dropped instantly, arrows protruding from their bodies. Others went down struggling to tear away the spears that had driven into them.

Tocoto glared around him in fury, then towards the white men who, exhausted though they were, had put a final spurt into running for the shelter of the buildings — and for some reason no attack was made on them. But it did continue to rain upon the natives, and Tocoto himself jumped in alarm as a poisoned arrow flicked close by his ear.

'Fight back, you fools!' he screamed to his own men. 'Fight back! You have the power of the jewel on your side.'

He was more or less wasting his time. The natives were assessing values by the amount of hurt they received and they did not like the idea of unseen 'hunters' raining destruction on them from the inaccessible fortresses on top of the buildings. Here and there the warriors threw spears back at their invisible aggressors, but it was a pitiful attempt. So they started to run, utterly demoralized, and a hail of arrows followed them, picking them off as they went. Slowly the darkening street became strewn with dead bodies, or those badly wounded. In the midst of them Tocoto stood gazing around him in furious bewilderment . . . then he too, started to move as arrows whanged dangerously close,

At last he turned and ran, away from the city, utterly beaten and boiling with fury. He knew whom to blame — the Untani tribe. The fact that they used arrows was proof of it. The Untani had always been a tribe intelligent beyond the ordinary and equipped with the most efficient weapons.

So Tocoto departed into the desert, to decide what he must do next. Bereft of all his black followers, and the white men, too, things had certainly not worked out as he had anticipated.

And whilst he slunk under the deepening night and decided what he should do next the few whites began investigating. Emerging from the shelter of the buildings into which they had hurried they found that no attack — as before

— was made upon them. Standing in a little ragged knot in the once main street of the city they waited as the natives began to come down in ever increasing numbers from the roof tops, until at last a full three score of them, armed to the teeth, had gathered.

'You are Untani tribe?' asked Robertson, the chief engineer of the Perrivale yacht, who had taken over such leadership as was required when Crespin had been wiped out.

'Untani,' assented one of the natives, in the tribe's tongue, which Robertson only just understood.

'But the last we saw of you, you had bolted after that attack Tocoto made. We thought you'd gone for good.'

'We went back home for more men, and found them. A little time after Tocoto attacked our kraal and killed most of our women. We saw it happen but did not hit back then. We heard Tocoto say many times that he would come to Akada, so we came ahead of him. When he arrived we avenged ourselves for his attack on our kraal.

Tocoto not yet dead, but we shall kill him yet.'

'Did you, in your travels, come across Anjani or Mrs. Perrivale?' Robertson asked, but the native shook his head in the starlight.

'Not see white lord Anjani or white woman. Not know where they are.'

'Then we have to find them, and you boys are just the ones to help us do it. Half of you should remain here and the other half go with us in an effort to find Anjani and the white woman. At sunrise, when we have rested. Is that understood?'

The black giant nodded and tapped his chest. 'You speak to Maloona,' he said. 'Maloona guide you. Maloona tribal chief and son of Miambo. Miambo slain and Maloona live only for revenge on Tocoto.'

Robertson nodded. 'I can understand that. We'll stay here for the night and start searching at sun-up. You might see what you can find for us in the way of food and drink. Tocoto didn't let us have much of either. We've a cache of supplies hidden between here and the coast, but have had no time to get at it. We'll do it later.'

Maloona gave orders to several of his men. Satisfied that, for the moment at least, they were safe enough, Robertson and his men retired to the nearest building, threw themselves down on the floor and relaxed. Only the need of food and drink kept them from falling instantly asleep.

★　★　★

Anjani, meantime, was on the move again, carrying the half sleeping Rita in a newly-fashioned 'cradle' as he glided through the night, searching constantly for the trail of Tocoto that he knew he must find someday. There were no signs of pursuit, the natives from Monango having evidently given up the idea, and the jungle was comparatively quiet in the moonlight. The only thing that worried Anjani was Rita's curious listlessness, following her ordeal in the arena. Usually a brief sleep refreshed her, but not this time. She hung heavy on his shoulders and seemed unable to arouse herself.

Half way through the night Anjani

paused and set the girl down in the cool undergrowth. A shaft of moonlight beaming through the treetops struck full upon her and what he saw worried Anjani a good deal. The girl was twisting and tossing uneasily in a half-coma. The only answer was that she had caught a tropical fever, possible through the lowering of her resistance during her experiences and the terrors she had undergone.

Anjani crouched in silence, not knowing what to do. He himself had never had the fever, but he had seen natives wiped out with it in a matter of hours. Sometimes it killed, sometimes not: it seemed to be up to the patient. The only thing Anjani did clearly understand was that this jungle was no place for a cure. The girl needed the free open air of a tableland, without the incessant swarms of disease-bearing insects and the dank vegetation. There was only one spot of which Anjani knew where the right conditions existed — the plateau and valley wherein Akada stood. As far as he could judge he was heading in its direction, but had not made any particular effort about it since the uppermost thought in his mind had been to pick up the trail of Tocoto. Now that no longer mattered: Rita had to be carried free of the jungle as quickly as possible.

Having made up his mind Anjani lifted the girl back into the shoulder cradle and began to get on the move again, completely tireless. He stopped only once at a jungle stream at which he moistened the girl's face and lips and drank deeply himself, then again he was on his wav, until by dawn he had picked up a familiar trail in the wilderness, which he knew led in the direction of the treasure city.

At dawn also Robertson and his men were awakened by Maloona to find he had brought in a breakfast in the shape of freshly killed and cooked small jungle animals. Robertson and his men, dirty and unshaven, ate hungrily and drank the coconut milk that had been provided. During this 'repast' Maloona looked on impassively, entirely conscious of his own responsibility now he was head of the much-decimated Untani tribe. Outside, all dead bodies had been removed.

'Safari ready, bwana,' he said presently, as Robertson cocked an enquiring eye towards him. 'Half my men stay here as you ordered; others try to pick up trail of Anjani the Mighty and the white woman. We ready to start.'

'Good enough,' Robertson acknowledged. 'What about Tocoto? Seen any sign of him?'

Maloona shook his head. 'Tocoto gone. Beaten. Back to jungle, perhaps.'

'Best place for him,' Robertson commented, getting to his feet. 'All right, Maloona, we're ready. Let's be going boys.'

Tocoto, though, was not so very far away. Still smarting from the defeat of the night and the loss of the men he had gathered after such ruthless tactics with the Akada jewel, he was more than ever determined to take revenge. Which was why he was only half a mile away from the city, lying out flat in the blaze of the morning, hidden by a tall rock. From his vantage point he could command a view of the entire city, and it was not long before he saw the party of blacks and white men departing, fully provisioned, and coming in his direction.

Tocoto counted the natives as near as be could, not in actual figures since he had no conception of mathematics but in visible quantity — and what he saw satisfied him that half at least were missing and must therefore be standing guard over Akada. Which, for the time being, banished all hope of perhaps getting more tribes to his banner and carrying out his original plans.

Not that Tocoto was particularly concerned any more about the treasures. He was beginning to believe, with the continued absence of Anjani and Rita, that both had been wiped out somewhere in the wilderness of the jungle. If so, there was not much point in trying to remove the treasure. On the other hand there was revenge to be taken for the onslaught the previous night . . .

Tocoto began edging around the rock as the party nearest him, so that he was kept constantly out of the line of vision. Finally he was to the rear of the party, watching it heading across the burning desert in the direction of the jungle. But why? This was the one thing Tocoto could not understand. If the Akada treasure was the main concern of the white men where was the sense of marching away from it? Somehow Tocoto realised, he had got to find out what was intended.

He waited until the party had almost become remote, then he rose from his hiding place and also headed for the jungle, but by a wide, roundabout route, which took him well out of range of those he was pursuing. He knew that once he had gained the jungle he would have no difficulty in discovering them.

In this he was correct. Towards noon, an hour after he had re-entered the primeval forest, he was moving silently through the treetops when he came upon the black and white party below, hacking its way laboriously through the vegetation. Every now and again one or other of the white men would cup his hands and call loudly — '*Anjani! Mrs. Perrivale!*'

Tocoto did not need any more obvious clue than this. He did not know the meaning of 'Mrs. Perrivale', but 'Anjani' made sense. Presumably there was a search for Anjani in progress, and this set Tocoto's wily mind to work. If a trail were found, a freshly made one, it was more than possible the party would follow it in the belief that it might lead them to Anjani.

Nothing easier than to make a trail, but it had to be in a certain place, and some distance away, so as to give the party time in which to reach it. There were preparations to be made.

Tocoto looked around him from his vantage point, noting which part of the jungle he was in — then, with a grim smile to himself, he sped silently ahead of the search party for a distance of perhaps two miles. Here he came upon the region for which he was looking — the bank of a small, swiftly flowing river. To the eye the bank was normal enough, but Tocoto knew differently, as did many of the jungle denizens. The bank in fact was treachery itself, undermined with water and of the consistency of quicksand. Sometimes an area was safe, sometimes not. To make sure of the area he wanted Tocoto tossed down a heavy piece of branch. The moment it struck the bank it began to sink, finally disappearing in yellow ooze.

Tocoto saw ahead of him the perfect revenge, and began to act fast. From his safe vantage point he lowered masses of vegetation to the bank, finally making it look as though leaves and small branches had dropped naturally. It hid the treachcrous area of the bank — a trap for the unwary.

This part of the plan complete he returned to the higher branches of the tree and then began to move quickly through the treetops until he again came upon the party cutting a way through the jungle. Moving back to some distance ahead of them he dropped to the ground, laid an obvious trail that they could not fail to follow, and finished it at the camouflaged river bank. Then he climbed back to a fork in the tree that overhung the danger area of the bank.

For a long time Tocoto sat waiting and listening, and presently the sound of knives on vegetation and the eager exchange of voices reached him. Though he could not understand what was being said he could gather that both whites and blacks believed they were following a genuine trail.

The natives, led by Maloona, reached the camouflaged area first. To Tocoto's annoyance the black giant paused, looking about him, one foot on the edge of the false undergrowth carpet.

'Trail stop here, bwana,' he said to Robertson. 'Maloona not understand. Trail should go on along bank.'

He pointed to the region beyond the vegetation where the bank appeared undisturbed. Tocoto wondered what had happened. In his eagerness to lay a trail to the danger area he had overlooked putting one beyond it.

'Are you sure we are following the trail of Anjani and maybe Mrs. Perrivale?' Robertson asked. 'Suppose it belongs to Tocoto? It could, just as easily.'

'We follow bank,' Maloona decided. 'Watch step, bwana. Many parts of bank dangerous.'

With that he strode forward and Tocoto grinned in satisfaction. Instantly the native was up to his knees in the mud as his feet went clean through the false undergrowth. He lunged forward, his hands plunging into the ooze so that he sank to his elbows. The men behind him, since they were strung out fairly widely, were also in the mire before they realised what had happened, but not all of them were involved — and the white men not at all since they were at the rear. They watched in horror for a moment as Maloona and six of his followers fought desperately to free themselves but only sank lower in the doing.

Tocoto chuckled and rubbed his hands.

'Bwana! Bwana!' Maloon shouted hoarsely. 'Devil mud!'

'Quick!' Robertson snapped to the men around him. 'Grab some tree branches and get these poor devils free.'

No time was wasted, but even so, Maloona sank a good deal lower in the interval, the ooze now up to his waist and pulling him down with relentless force. The five natives around him slapped and struggled against the filth, unaware that the more they struggled the less chance they stood. Finally they could only look imploringly at Robertson, his colleagues, and the rest of the Untani as they did their best to reach out with tree branches. Maloona grabbed hold of one of them and held on to it frantically as five natives pulled desperately to free him.

He partly came out, then the branch snapped and he fell abruptly on his face. Robertson jerked his eyes away with horror, for there was nothing the hapless native could do to save himself. Doubled up as he was he could not drag clear and his back and hands vanished slowly leaving behind a bubble of yellow liquid.

The remaining natives began screaming for help, the mud halfway up their broad chests. Another branch was brought and held out to them, but hard though it was pulled the mud was a stronger master, and the natives went down slowly — chest, shoulders, neck, until finally they were gone.

'This is hell,' Robertson whispered, shaken. 'No man could have crossed this plague spot. The trail must have been a false one — maybe an animal or something.'

'Trail made by man,' declared one of the Untani stubbornly.

'Then he must have taken to the treetops,' Robertson said. 'Which means it was probably Tocoto. Maybe he laid this on purpose — Anyway, let's get out. Nothing we can do here.'

So the party turned and began moving back through the forest, casting around for possible new trails and sobered by the ghastly fate that had overtaken the new chief of the tribe and six of his picked warriors.

Tocoto saw them go and scowled in annoyance. Seven was not many to have wiped out in revenge for the previous night. Perhaps there were other snares he could devise — hanging vines which could lift one or other of the men by the neck and kill them, or maybe lions could be led into their path —

Tocoto broke off his speculations and turned sharply as he heard a sound in the tree behind him. He was just in time to see two enormous green eyes fixed on him balefully, to see a magnificent spotted body dappled with the sunlight between the leaves — then the leopard, which had crept upon him so quietly suddenly sprang.

Tocoto did not stand a chance. Even as he flashed his hand down to his knife the leopard knocked him flying from the tree branch, straight down into the yellow ooze below. He landed feet first as chance had it, and immediately began to sink. Unable to save itself the leopard slithered from the branch too and dropped with a resounding splash in the mud. It lashed out with its claws towards the struggling Tocoto and then could do no more as the mud dragged it down relentlessly. It lashed and struggled and spat madly, but it had no chance in the relentless syrup. Down it went, tail first, the magnificent head going last in a turgid eddy of bubbles.

Already sunk to his waist Tocoto still kept his wits about him and glanced anxiously around for something he could seize. The tree was not far away, from which he had fallen, and he made one flailing effort to grab its lower branches — and missed by inches. The second time the inches had widened considerably and there was nothing he could do. He began to become alarmed, the mud rising above his waist and tearing at his feet.

Finally he screamed for help. Even if the black and white party heard him and came back he did not care: they were fools enough to save him even though he was an enemy. But evidently they were out of earshot, for nothing happened. Tocoto sank lower, the mud-level just under his muscular breasts. He grabbed hold of the false undergrowth he had spread around, but it sank instantly —

Then to his infinite relief there were sounds of smashing vegetation in the nearby jungle. He watched intently, and despite his predicament found time to be surprised as he beheld a score or so of natives, smaller than normal, bearing black and white ivory spears in their hands. He found it impossible to place them, but that fact did not signify at the moment.

The blacks held a hurried consultation, then Tocoto found one of the spears held out to him. He grasped it, but the united strength of three of the natives was insufficient to drag him free. So a different move was made. Two of the natives hurried around the rim of the swamp, quickly climbed to the lower fork branch of the tree where Tocoto himself had been concealed, and then they edged themselves out along it. Finally they locked their knees over the outer branch and swung head downwards, their powerful hands reaching out until they had each gripped Tocoto by an arm. They pulled with all their power and he himself struggled to drag upwards.

There was a sucking of ooze and he came partly free. Still the natives persisted, both of them gymnasts from the party that had 'entertained' High Chieftainess Mea before her death. Tocoto rose a bit higher. Each native held him now by his armpits and was pulling furiously. On the edge of the area other natives were reaching out as far as they dared, held by their fellows, until the outermost leaning one had gripped him round the waist. The rest was a tug-of-war between the warriors and the mud, and at last Tocoto was dragged free and deposited, gasping, on the undergrowth. By the time he had got to his feet and cleaned away the clinging ooze with leaves the natives were around him in a circle, cold menace in their eyes.

'You speak my tongue?' Tocoto asked, in the tribal language.

Apparently not. The reply that the leader of the party gave was difficult for Tocoto to understand, but here and there words made sense.

'You — stole. Jewel of Akada!' The black reached forward and with a sudden wrench snapped the thong of the bag Tocoto had about his neck. Tocoto clenched his fists but did not dare try anything with the spears so close to him.

'Me — Barmono,' the native said. 'We seek — much distance. Find white giant like you, and white woman. They fled into jungle. We find him and kill: Terrible Highness die because of him. But you real thief of Akada. We kill you — and other white man.'

'You could have left me in the swamp,' Tocoto retorted. 'Why save me to kill me. It makes no sense.'

'Barmono take you to Akada,' the black answered. 'You put jewel back. Then we kill.'

He shook the jewel from the bag and studied it as it lay in his palm. Then he handed it, with the bag, to the native standing next to him, presumably for safe keeping on the journey.

Tocoto looked from one to the other in bewilderment. Not knowing the facts about Monango or what had happened there he was in a complete daze, particularly as these natives were so unlike any he had ever encountered before. About the only thing that did make sense to him was the information that Anjani and Rita Perrivale were still alive, and presumably somewhere in the forest.

'March!' Barmono ordered, with a quick motion of his hand — and Tocoto had to obey. He was resolved that before

Akada was reached he would find some way of escaping — but in that he greatly underestimated the vigilance of the men of Monango.

6

Mutiny

Robertson and the men of the Untani grouped around him and his white colleagues were two miles from the quicksand region when a halt was called.

'This is useless,' Robertson declared. 'We find not the least clue as to the whereabouts of Mrs. Perrivale and Anjani and we'll probably only run into fresh dangers if Tocoto is watching us. We must call the search off and return to Akada, then load up as much treasure as we can find and get out. There's nothing else for it. We'll pick up that cache of stores, too.'

The men around him nodded, only too glad of the chance to abandon the jungle and make a bid for leaving Africa. Just the same, Robertson's conscience was giving him a few twinges because he still could not rid himself of the conviction that Rita Perrivale was alive *somewhere*, and he knew too, that Captain Hart would not take kindly to the notion of giving up the search. On the other hand there were limits to the endurance of the white men and the dangers they could face.

'I think,' Robertson added, looking at the waiting natives, 'that you boys, and those who have been left at Akada, had better join forces when we get back. All of you can start a search, much better able to do it than us. While you are about it the rest: of us will carry on to the coast and advise Captain Hart of what's happened and see what he suggests. We can't start moving the treasure until we get a clear sanction from him.'

Though he didn't understand completely, the native who had taken Maloona's place in a position of authority gave a quick nod.

'Me and rest of men search, bwana. As you say. We take you back to Akada first.'

'Good enough,' Robertson acknowledged. 'Let's go.'

And the journey resumed, on through the interminable forest, dodging its dangers, pausing only when the heat became so intense that the white men just had to rest. And nowhere in their travels did they pick up the least clue concerning Rita or Anjani. So, finally, after another night and a day, detouring only to the cache, they came within sight of the lost city once more.

They found it undisturbed when they reached it, the natives they had left behind still on guard. Robertson's first move was to return to the quarters he and his men had made for themselves in the city centre then he transferred authority to the native who had taken Maloona's place,

'Take all your men,' he instructed, 'and comb out the jungle in every possible direction. In any case return here when you have finished; and if we have not returned from the coast remain here until we do. If you should find the white woman or Anjani keep them here until that time. You understand that?'

Umkangi nodded his woolly head. 'Umkangi go,' he said, and left the big stone apartment with its assortment of camp-beds and various provisions.

Robertson moved to the glassless window and stood watching in the evening sunlight as the natives prepared for departure. Half-an-hour later they were on their way in double-file, heading out across the desert.

'When do we start for the coast, Mr. Robertson?' one of the men asked, busy setting out canned food from the stores.

'Sun-up.' Robertson turned back into the room and massaged his aching back. 'Spend tonight here, then be on our way.'

'I suppose you realise, chief, that we're left without any protection?' another of the men asked dubiously.

'As far as natives are concerned, yes — but we have rifles and plenty of ammunition if there's any trouble, and this room wouldn't be tough to hold against an army of natives. They only have the advantage when they can sneak up outside. In any event, even if I've taken a risk I think those natives are better looking for Mrs. Perrivale than standing guard over us.'

That ended the matter. Robertson was in charge and therefore could not be questioned. The men settled down their meal as the sunlight died, washing the food down with the contents of their water bottles. By the time they had finished the brief twilight had closed into night and Akada was silent as the tomb.

'Makes you think,' one of the men mused, sprawled on his blankets and smoking irritatingly dry tobacco. 'We're stuck here with a fortune worth millions and we've all the sweat and grind and danger to ship it back to civilization — and we get nothing out of it but wages. And who gets the money? If not Mrs. Perrivale — who is worth fifty million at least — then some damned relative of hers who is already soaked to the gills in money.'

'You can cut that sort of talk,' Robertson snapped. 'We came here under an agreement and we stick to it. I don't think we'll be left with just our wages after all we've gone through. This is no ordinary trading job.'

'You're telling us,' another man grunted, and then he settled down to sleep.

Robertson did not say any more. He sat

smoking his harsh pipe and thinking — not without worry. The men were obviously finding the thought of so much treasure close at hand almost too much for them. There might even be mutiny later. The best of men had been known to throw scruples overboard for far less. Robertson wished devoutly that he had had First Mate Crespin with him: there were few men who had been able to handle men as he could —

A sound came on Robertson's ears as he sat thinking, his back to the wall. He glanced up, not sure if he had really heard it — then it came again and it sounded almost like a human cry for help. Immediately he was on his feet and those men around him who were not asleep rose too. They hurried to the door of the building and looked outside.

'There!' Robertson exclaimed suddenly. 'Down the street!'

The men around him peered into the uncertain starlight, hands on their guns, then gradually they descried what had already become apparent to Robertson's sharper eyes.

Against the white dust of the street a figure was visible, bearing another figure in his arms. He was moving unsteadily and seemed to be at the point of exhaustion. As he came nearer, looking about him, Robertson gave a gasp.

'Hell's devils, it's Anjani! Carrying Mrs. Perrivale! Quick, give him a hand.'

There was no hesitation. All the white men, for the remainder had been aroused by now, hurried forward, and caught at Anjani's mighty form as he reeled and tottered with Rita in his arms. She was taken from him and borne quickly away, then he steadied himself for a moment and breathed hard, looking at the dim faces.

'I was not sure if anybody was here,' he explained, his chest heaving. 'I — I have been travelling without a stop for many days and nights. Rita is ill with fever and — and I do not know how to cure her.'

'We do,' Robertson said briefly. 'Come in and rest and have some food. I didn't think a man like you could ever be exhausted!'

'Four days and nights without sleep is a

long time,' Anjani muttered. 'I — I had to. I fear for Rita. She is so ill.'

He walked with the little knot of men down the street, and into the building they were occupying. The oil lamp — which they had not been using for fear of giving away their position to possible native prowlers — was now lighted and its dim yellow glow cast on Rita as she lay on blankets, tossing and turning and muttering to herself, her face flushed and dewed.

'Uh-huh, she's got it all right,' Robertson commented. 'Fortunately we've all the drugs necessary to put her right, if she isn't too far gone. Briggs, get the first-aid kit over here. Saunders, see Anjani gets a meal and water.'

Both orders were obeyed, and under the influence of the food and water Anjani began to quickly recover. Meanwhile he crouched and watched Robertson at work. He did not understand what was being done, but at least he knew it was for the best and let it go at that.

'Nothing we can do now except let Nature take its course,' Robertson said, standing up. 'We'll rig a net over this bed and keep a watch. I think she'll be all right, but it will take a day or two.'

'Does that matter, so long as she recovers?' Anjani asked.

'No — but it does hold us up. We shan't be able to move from here until she is completely well again, and that may be some time.'

Ajani shrugged, not seeing that it signified. Robertson, however, did not like the idea of staying too long in Akada. He still was not sure what Tocoto was up to, and whether or not he might not spring a devastating surprise at any moment. The way things were, apparently, there was nothing for it but to stay.

'You have no Untani here?' Anjani asked at length. 'I did not see them anywhere.'

'They're in the jungle, Anjani, looking for you and Mrs. Perrivale. It may be some days before they return. We can't move any treasure until then. I'd planned to return to the yacht and ask Captain Hart if we should move the treasure in Mrs. Perrivale's absence. Now she has returned the trip is unnecessary. We just sit here and wait until the Untani come back with their story of failure.'

'I still have Tocoto to find,' Anjani muttered. 'When Rita is well again I shall set off to find him. I was going to do so when she was taken ill. Since then I have thought of nothing but getting her out of the jungle to fresher air — You are sure she will recover?' he asked anxiously.

'No reason why not,' Robertson answered, watching as a fine net was rigged up over the makeshift bed.

Satisfied that all that could be done had been done, Anjani moved over to a spot by the wall, relaxed, and within a few minutes was asleep. Robertson looked at his men in the dim light.

'We'll be here indefinitely,' he said. 'Like the rest of you I'd rather hoped we had a good excuse to get on the move, but now it's gone.'

And that, as far as he was concerned, ended the matter. He detailed one of the men to keep watch over Rita in case she recovered from her feverish delirium and needed something; the others settled

146

down to get some sleep.

Out in the jungle the warriors of Monango were also sleeping, most of them anyway. Two remained alert, close to Tocoto, wary for anything he might attempt. Just the same, their vigilance was not quite so keen as it might have been. For three nights they had kept watch over the white giant and he had hardly stirred, so there seemed no reason why he should do so this night in particular. In consequence the men were considerably off guard, seated near Tocoto and with their spears within reach. He himself was wide awake even though simulating deep slumber. He had waited patiently for this chance, when the watch on him would be at its lowest ebb.

Tocoto peered around him in the gloom. The rest of the Monango warriors were some distance away, most of them asleep around a low-burning fire, To Tocoto's rear was the jungle which, once he reached it, would be complete cover for him. So he began to prepare himself to move. When he felt the moment was propitious he suddenly leapt to his feet and made one dive for the nearby screen of trees. He would doubtless have made his getaway successfully had not a prowling lion happened to emerge at that moment, barring his path. He veered to one side, pursued by the natives. They hesitated for a moment at the sight of the hungry carnivore, and the next thing Tocoto knew he had been knocked off his feet by a blow of the springing creature's paw.

Lacerated down the back Tocoto flung up his hands and buried them in the tawny throat, forcing the slavering jaws away from his face. With his feet he kicked savagely into the lion's belly. Unarmed, there were no other tactics he could adopt. Indeed he was all prepared to fight to the death, since this was what he expected the warriors would allow to happen — but to his surprise spears were hurled into the furious beast until at last it sagged helplessly, dying, pinning Tocoto under its great weight. He pulled himself from beneath it and stood up, wincing at the pain of his gashed back and feeling the stickiness of blood coursing down it.

'You unwise,' Barmono spat at him. 'Try to make escape. Barmono not like that. For the rest of the march you shall be tied.'

He added brief orders to his men and the next thing Tocoto knew was that his wrists had been drawn immovably behind him with thin vine-thong and his ankles were hobbled. The fact that his back was deeply scored from claw marks did not seem to matter in the least to his captors. So, furious with himself at his failure to escape — which chance had now forever gone — he spent the rest of the night twinging with pain and feeling blood dry hard upon him.

When the day came his weariness and pain were disregarded. He was given a meagre meal for a breakfast and then forced on the march again. At first he thought he would never be able to maintain the wearying, enervating journey — but as the day wore on he began to recover again, unaware that his strength was returning as he replaced the blood he had lost. Now and again, during pauses, his wrists were untied and at these times he made it an excuse to seize the nearest green leaves he could find and hold them to the wounds in his back.

'Lion helped us,' Barmono commented cynically, as he watched Tocoto tending to himself. 'Barmono believe now that there are two men — you and other man. Scars on your back will make us able to know you. Other man never be mistaken for you again.'

'Since you plan to kill me anyway I don't see the advantage,' Tocoto retorted.

'We make sure. The gods smile on you perhaps and you escape. We always know you by scars.'

Tocoto said no more but his glance was bitter. As far as he could estimate Akada would he reached by the time the day's march was over, and unless he thought of something very quickly it would probably also mean the end of his life. But with feet hobbled and wrists once again secured behind him there was just nothing at all he could devise to get away. So, presently, the march continued . . .

And in Akada, thanks to the drugs Robertson had given her, Rita was showing the first signs of recovery. The actual fever had left her and she was entirely rational, but completely weakened. Since there were none of the building-up foods he would have liked, Robertson used canned meat in boiling water to make a broth. It was simple, very ordinary fare, but at least it helped Rita to rebuild her strength.

Constantly watching over her was Anjani, he himself now completely recovered after his night's sleep. For the rest of the men there was very little to do except wander about the city, think of the treasure it contained, and then wonder how long it would be before the Untani returned from their now needless mission.

'What happens,' one of them asked Robertson, 'if those natives take weeks to come back? They might, since you told them to search thoroughly.'

'We wait,' Robertson answered. 'Nothing else we can do. We can't move all this heavy ivory and gold by ourselves: that's the very reason for having the Untani, so they can aid us.'

'I maintain they are not really needed,' another of the men said. 'They'll be useful if we plan to make the trip back to the steamer at one go — but otherwise I don't see why we can't move the stuff ourselves by making several journeys. It's about two days' march to the coast. Just sticking around here waiting for something to happen is sheer murder.'

Robertson considered for a moment. 'I'll see Mrs. Perrivale,' he said, and walked across to the building where he had his headquarters.

As usual he found Anjani seated on the blankets near the girl, ready to provide anything she needed. The jungle man looked up questioningly as Robertson came in and Rita turned her head wearily.

'I hate bothering you at a time like this, madam, but I think I should,' Robertson apologised. 'I'm having trouble with the men. Probably the climate, the fear of attack, and a hundred and one other causes — but they want to be moving.'

'That's ridiculous, Mr. Robertson,' Rita answered, her voice low. 'They were employed for no other reason than to help move the treasure — and we will when the Untani men come back.'

'I know; but I think we could save ourselves a lot of trouble if I allowed the men to start moving the ivory and gold on their own account. If they're kept busy they'll be all right. Idling about puts ideas in their heads.'

'Very well then. The treasure has to be moved, whoever does it. Just carry on, Mr. Robertson. You know how to handle men better than I do.'

'I think I should go with them. I don't trust a single mother's son of them with that much ivory and gold among them.'

Rita nodded. 'Best of luck, Mr. Robertson.'

'There's one thing else bothering me . . . ' Robertson had a troubled smile, then as Rita gave him an inquiring glance he added, 'I feel badly about having to leave you and Anjani here by yourselves, unprotected.'

'You needn't,' Anjani said dryly. 'I can take care of Rita, and myself, no matter what happens.'

'Even against Tocoto? Remember, he is

somewhere in the jungle and may eventually get this far with some tribe or other to aid him. If that happened — '

'My one ambition in life is to get to grips with Tocoto again,' Anjani broke in. 'I'll take care of the situation, believe me. You see to your men or you'll have trouble.'

'Very well,' Robertson assented. 'We'll start getting the first load of treasure ready immediately.'

He departed actively and it was two hours later when he returned, grimy and perspiring, to announce that he was ready to go. All Rita could do was shake hands weakly, but Anjani went out into the street to watch the men depart, carrying as much ivory as they could between them and fully provided with necessities for the march. They left the main street amidst a haze of dust, striking out for the rugged land that led to the distant coast.

Anjani looked about him for a moment on the utter desertion and the distant jungle, then he turned back into the building and resumed his position at Rita's side.

'Seems more natural this way,' he said. 'You and I left together, I mean. That is how we seem to spend most of our lives.'

Rita smiled a little, then it was replaced by a troubled frown. Her hot, restless hand settled on Anjani's forearm.

'There may have been something in what Robertson said, you know,' she reflected. 'About Tocoto, I mean. Just suppose he does suddenly make an attack and is helped by scores of tribesmen. Just what will you do to defeat him?'

'Fight back,' Anjani answered simply. 'I know no other law — or way.'

'But you haven't the weapons — not to fight a horde, anyway. Just a spear and the rifles Robertson has left behind.'

Anjani glanced towards the open doorway. Then he said:

'This room can be made a stronghold, little one, once the door is shut. The window can become the spot from which I can attack. Which reminds me I know nothing of the weapon that spits death. Perhaps I had better examine it?'

'Be careful!' Rita warned in alarm, as he got up. 'If you investigate too much you may kill yourself! Bring a rifle to me and I'll show you what to do.'

Anjani nodded and brought the weapon over. Rita lay and began to give instructions.

'Put the wooden part against your shoulder. Anjani — Yes, that's it. No, the other shoulder since you're right-handed. Now, that's the trigger — Yes, there. Go to the window and do as I tell you. You'll find the wooden part will kick back onto your shoulder when you put pressure on the trigger . . . Now, get your target in the rear-sight — yes, that's it — and bring the foresight up to match — Got it? Now!'

Interested in the experiment Anjani did as ordered and put gentle pressure on the trigger. A second later the bullet exploded against the wall of the building opposite and the echoes of the shot resounded through the deserted city.

'Tocoto will not stand much chance with this when I have learned properly,' he said, glancing back at the girl. 'What do I do now?'

'Bring it back to me and I'll show you . . . '

The shot had been heard in more places than Akada, though. Robertson and his men, crossing the dusty, sun-blistered waste towards the coast, all heard it and came to a stop. They looked at one another — then there came more distant shots.

'Come on,' Robertson said abruptly. 'Something's wrong. I knew I should never have left them — '

He began to stride forward, but none of the burdened men attempted to follow him. Grim-faced, he returned to them and cuffed up his sun helmet.

'What's the matter?' he demanded. 'Didn't you hear what I said?'

Big Joe, one of the yacht's stokers, spat leisurely.

'We heard — sure thing, but we're not going. If Mrs. Perrivale has got herself tied up with trouble she can stop that way. I haven't much time for women with millions, or men who live in the jungle, either.'

'You listen to me,' Robertson said deliberately. 'I left rifles behind so those two could protect themselves. That they are firing now is sure proof of trouble and it's our duty to — '

He stopped, looking grimly in the direction of the distant city as there were two more reports.

'It's our duty to look after ourselves,' Big Joe said sourly. 'And now seems as good a time as any to tell yon something, Mr. Chief Engineer. Me and the boys arrived at the conclusion some time ago that it's one hell of a waste for all this ivory and gold — and what's left of it in Akada — to be going to a woman who's already got more money than she can stagger about with. So we're taking it, see? We've enough here to satisfy us and keep us comfortable for a long time to come. Rest of our lives, maybe.'

'Stop talking like a fool!' Robertson blazed. 'How the devil do you ever suppose you can ship that stuff to England — or even to *anywhere* — without being questioned?'

'We're on the coast of Africa, where traders are thicker than tsetse flies,' Big Joe retorted. 'We don't aim to ship the stuff but to sell it to a trader right here in this country — and we won't have no difficulty. Ivory or gold fetch their price anywhere. We've the whole run of the coast from Nyanga to Walvis Bay and we'll find a buyer without going anywhere near the Perrivale yacht or the tramp.'

Robertson breathed hard. 'And when you try and return for more treasure? How do you propose to do that?'

'We shan't return, Chief; we're not that crazy. I just said, didn't I, we've enough with us to turn in enough money to suit? Seems to me,' Big Joe added, with a glance at his colleagues, 'that it's time to tell Mr. Robertson a few things, isn't it?'

'More'n time!'

'Tell him, Joe.'

'You're the one likely to upset our plans,' Big Joe explained. 'We'd only one aim when we said we wanted to be on the move, and that was to get some of this stuff for ourselves. We've done it — and we're glad you came too because it makes it easier.'

Robertson dropped his hand to his gun, realising he ought to have done it much sooner. He did not draw, however, for Joe's gun was already levelled.

'Disarm him, Cliff,' Joe ordered, and another of the men promptly relieved the chief engineer of his only weapon.

'In other words, robbery and murder?' he asked slowly. 'I wouldn't have thought it of you, Big Joe. I know you haven't a very good record but I didn't include this sort of mutiny in my speculations — '

'Aw, shut up! We're men, ain't we? We're entitled to take a fortune same as anybody else. Mrs. Millions Perrivale isn't thinking twice about emptying Akada, is she? Why should we?'

'There are certain laws, Joe, and she has it all legally arranged. Something to do with salvage, and — '

'We've as much right to it as she has and we're taking it. And you're not going to get the chance to talk, either. Start marching, Chief.'

Robertson did as he was told, his face hard as he thought the matter out. In many ways he could not blame the men. He had seen even better men go completely to the bad when faced with incomparable wealth. His main concern now was his own safety. In his present mood Big Joe was not likely to pull his punches . . . Nor did he. Perhaps five miles further on a halt was called in a wooded outcropping.

'This'll do,' Joe said, and evidently understanding what he meant his colleagues put down their heavy loads and heaved thankful sighs that they were in the shade of trees for a while.

'Since we could hear those shots from Akada where we were, they could probably have heard my gun too,' the stoker explained, still with his weapon in his hand. 'This far away they never will.'

Robertson clenched his fists, his heart thudding. By the merciless glint in Big Joe's eyes he knew what was coming.

'Look, Joe,' Robertson said, trying to keep his voice steady, 'what's it worth to you to turn yourself into a killer? You'll never get away with that ivory. Traders are not fools. For their own sake they'll make enquiries and — '

The stoker's gun fired — twice. Robertson went down without a sound and lay still in the sandy soil. The men looked at each other as Joe slowly reholstered his weapon.

'He'd have been a nuisance,' he said. 'An' we can't afford a nuisance between us and a fortune. From now on, boys, we're on our own — and we're wasting time. Less any of you feels too weak to carry on?'

That was quite sufficient to get the men shouldering their burdens again, completely relying on Big Joe to finish the course of mutiny and theft he had started.

'It'll be another day at least before we sight the coast,' he said. 'When that happens we keep a watch for where the yacht and steamer are, then we head due north from them. That ought to bring us to Nyanga. We can do business there.'

The men nodded, entirely in agreement. It would be worth the arduous march and the blinding sunlight to have a fortune at the end of it, and since the fortune could only come if all the ivory were delivered there with no chance of one man doing a double-cross and running off with the lot. Taken all in all, everything seemed set fair for a life of ease and plenty, once Nyanga was reached.

But between the toiling men and Nyanga lay a treacherous route and not one of them knew exactly where they were . . .

* * *

By nightfall Ajani was a passably good shot — good enough anyway to protect himself against unwary savages. Against an expert gunman he would not have stood a chance.

He gave up his practise as the night began to close down and, as a precaution, closed the door of the big lower room and dropped the stone bar across it; then he lighted the oil lamp and carried it over to where Rita was lying. She gave him a smile, the brightest he had seen so far. Throughout the day she had been making steady progress, thanks to makeshift soup and small meals and drinks at intervals.

'I'm never anything else but a nuisance, am I?' she asked gently, as Anjani's big arm settled behind her shoulders and raised her a little.

'Not to me,' he murmured.

'But for me I believe that by now everything would have gone according to plan. I've delayed things by becoming ill. I — '

'The very strongest get ill sometimes,' Anjani broke in. 'I cannot see it matters now you are recovering, and we are together. We could not be closer even if we were in civilization . . . '

He stopped, his voice sinking into quiet. Rita recognised what it meant. He had heard something with his uncannily quick ears.

'What?' she asked, tensing a little.

'Sounds — outside. Still a way off.'

Anjani got to his feet, and sped quickly across the great room. He did not trouble to unfasten the door; instead he vaulted lightly through the glassless window, and then looked up and down the narrow vista between buildings. The sounds came to him more clearly now, but he could not see the source of them, so he moved to the main street. From here he could dimly discern what had caught his attention — a still fairly distant crowd of natives, it seemed to be, with one white figure in their midst. The rising moonlight and Anjani's keen night sight were sufficient to show that much.

Immediately he hurried back to the anxious Rita and found her making shaky efforts to rise from the bed. He gently forced her down to it again.

'You're far too weak for that,' he told her.

'I — I know, but I was worried. If you hadn't come back — What did you see?'

Anjani blew out the flame of the oil lamp. 'I think Tocoto is coming,' he murmured, picking up the rifle from beside him. 'And with him are perhaps two score or so of natives. The very thing Robertson thought would happen has come about.'

'Tocoto!' Rita gasped, horrified. 'But — but, Anjani, you can never fight him and a host of natives as well!'

'I'm going to try,' he answered simply, patting the rifle. 'If I don't win I'll at least give them a surprise.'

He turned to the window and remained crouched there, waiting. He knew that if

Tocoto and his 'men' were aware of his presence here they would first try the door — then come to the window when they found the door barred, and that was the moment Anjani was waiting for . . . but to his growing surprise nothing happened. Akada remained completely silent. Finally he raised himself and looked out of the window into the night. Nothing was happening.

At length he turned back to the girl, watching anxiously from the bed.

'I don't understand it,' he confessed. 'I could have sworn I saw Tocoto and a group of natives approaching. The only explanation is that they have perhaps gone to the treasure vault, not even bothering to look — '

'Then that makes us safe,' Rita said, relieved. 'They may not even bother to look — '

'But you do not suppose I am going to allow Tocoto to come this close and yet do nothing about it?' Anjani broke in, surprised. 'I'm going to find him, Rita, and settle things for all time.'

'But you *can't*! Please, Anjani, listen to

me. Even with that rifle you'll stand no chance against so many — '

'I'm going.' he declared stubbornly 'Tocoto is at last within arm's reach and that's all I need. I'll do better without this gun, so you'd better take it for protection while I am gone. Have no fear: I shall return safely.'

Again Rita tried entreaties, but he would not listen. He left the rifle within reach of her hand, vaulted lightly through the window and dropped into the night. Afterwards, as silent as a shadow, he began investigating.

He headed directly for the treasure-vault, expecting that would be the one place to look. And he was correct. The huge stone, which normally barred the way to the underground treasure-vault had been moved aside, just as Robertson and his men had left it. Anjani smiled to himself, crept down the narrow, vegetation-lined slope, and was swallowed up in the blackness of the tunnel that led into the cave of ivory and gold.

As he advanced into the depths he could hear the sound of a man's voice speaking in a tribal tongue, and it brought him up sharp, frowning. It was no ordinary tribal jargon to which he was listening but the language of the natives of Monango.

' . . . you return jewel to rock where it stood,' the voice was saying. 'Here, take it in your hand. And you are warned, white thief, that if you make one false move you will be killed instantly. Once you have returned the stone the sacrificial rites will begin.'

Puzzled, Anjani moved forward again. He could not fathom how Tocoto came to be mixed up with the men of Monango, unless they had made a mistake in identity. Then, as he came round the bend in the tunnel, Anjani came suddenly upon a surprising scene.

Tocoto was present in the centre of the natives of Monango, many of them holding flickering torches. To the rear loomed the great masses of ivory and gold. And, to one side of Tocoto, the low spur of rock with a flat top, which evidently was the normal resting place for the jewel. Tocoto took it into his hand from the black chief and studied it. It cast back the torchlight in blood-red glimmerings.

'Obey!' the chief snapped.

Tocoto did so and then turned again, his fists clenched. Anjani remained silent, in the deepest shadow, watching. It was commencing to occur to him that in his eagerness to find his brother he had neglected to remember that he was unarmed. Formerly he had a spear replacing his knife: now he had not even got a spear in case it encumbered his movements. He had little doubt that his bare hands could deal with Tocoto, but the natives with their ivory spears were a different proposition.

In any event Tocoto looked likely to be wiped out for having stolen the jewel, so Anjani began to withdraw silently. He would wait at the entrance to the treasure vault and see if the men of Monango emerged *without* Tocoto; if so they would have saved him a great deal of trouble.

But he had reckoned without the rat that suddenly scampered across his foot and startled him. Involuntarily he made a noise and the natives immediately detected it and looked up sharply. Anjani started running as his only escape but before he had reached the tunnel mouth strong hands had seized him. He slammed up his fists violently and sent two of the blacks reeling, but that was as far as he got. His hands were seized and forced behind him and the points of spears were within an inch of his broad chest,

'Killer of Mea!' Barmono cried fiercely. 'The gods smile upon us. The thief of Akada and the killer of Mea together.'

Anjani struggled savagely, but was quite unable to prevent himself being dragged into the treasure cave where his brother stood watching. They looked at each other.

'You both die!' Barmono declared, exultant. 'But not by the spear . . . You will fight, white giants, and the winner also shall die. How much more interesting to see you destroy each other, than for us to do it. Take them outside!' he finished curtly.

The warriors obeyed, and to force two such powerful men down the tunnel was no easy task, but finally — still held tightly — Anjani and Tocoto emerged under the stars.

'Street in middle of town,' Barmono instructed. 'Let them fight there, where they have room. We watch in circle.'

His followers nodded and Anjani and Tocoto were pushed along suddenly, only being released when the main street of Akada had been gained and the warriors had formed a tight circle, their spears ready.

'Fight!' Barmono commanded, grinning. 'Let us see the white lords destroy each other.'

Anjani gave his brother a grim look, then he said:

'Though I dislike being ordered what to do by these men of Monango, nothing could please me better than the chance to finish off the struggle we started when the bull-ape kidnapped Rita. I'll fight you, Tocoto, and kill you.'

'After which, *you* will die,' Tocoto answered, in the same tribal tongue. 'You heard what Barmono said. With only death as the reward for fighting, where is the reason in fighting at all?'

'I shall fight for the personal revenge I intend to take on you,' Anjani retorted. 'For the destruction of the village of the Untani — for many things!'

'Fight!' Barmono screamed, weary of arguments. 'Fight, or die where you stand . . . '

Anjani clenched his fists and prepared for action; then he glanced up at the sound of heavy stone rattling and thudding. It was coming from the door of the dwelling where he had left Rita. The natives looked in its direction, motionless as the small figure of Rita became visible. She had distinctly heard the voices in the main street and, weary though she was, could not remain immobile in bed whilst the voices in the main street continued.

In a matter of moments she had grasped the situation and put the heavy rifle to her shoulder. Her probable intention was to fire it, but she just had not the strength to do so. She swayed dizzily, dropped the weapon, then caught at the door-edge to save herself. By this time two of the men of Monango had reached her, hauling her forward until she was directly in front of the grim-faced Barmono.

'Hold her!' he commanded. 'She too has a penalty to pay for cheating Simbalo of the sacrifice and for helping the white giant against unhappy Mea.'

Anjani swung, hot words ready — then he remembered that Tocoto was there by reason of the terrific uppercut that struck him under the jaw. He staggered, then collapsed flat on his back with Tocoto on top of him.

7

Fight to the death

Big Joe and his followers, never sure but what something might catch up with them at any moment, wasted little time that night in resting. They paused for three hours, all told, in sections, sleeping in turns, then pushing on through the darkness, anxious to hit the coastline and be rid of their heavy burdens.

As by day they had used the sun as their compass, so now they used the stars and constantly headed westwards. The going was more or less easy until they came to a semi-mountainous region that preceded the actual barren land and sandy desert leading to the coast itself.

In fact, they were following a route that Anjani had been careful to avoid when he had taken Rita to the coastline. There were short, level cuts through the frowning walls — but of these the men with the ivory on their shoulders knew nothing, so exhausted though they were becoming they toiled up rocky acclivities and down slopes, always hoping that the next bend would bring them within sight of level land and distant sea.

No such thing happened, and they kept on toiling steadily, checking their route by the stars ever and again, hardly bothering to speak to one another. They had descended from a high ridge to a narrow, rocky bowl when a sound stopped them. It was a curious deep hissing note.

'What the hell was that?' one of the men demanded. 'Sounded like a snake to me.'

'Too loud,' Big Joe said, listening.

They all became silent again, puzzled as they looked about them. The hissing note came again after a while and was apparently some distance ahead in the narrow area into which they had come.

'Have to keep going,' Big Joe said. 'Whatever it is we'll deal with it.'

So they went on again in the starlight, and the more they advanced the more they became aware of ever-increasing heat. In any case the air was hot enough, but it seemed here to have become completely intolerable. Again came the hissing — nearer and louder this time.

'I get it!' Big Joe exclaimed suddenly, an edge of alarm in his voice. 'This region's volcanic. That's what all the heat is about. As for the hissing, maybe it's a crater or a blow-hole in the ground, or something — '

He broke off, or rather his words were completely drowned out, for at that moment the hissing ahead increased to the din of a dozen steam-jets, nearly splitting the eardrums with its intensity. At the same moment several of the men howled with pain as scalding steam and spray descended on them.

'A geyser!' one of them yelled, stumbling back and dropping his load. 'Boiling water and big as hell — '

He began running, and only a second or two later the rest of the men ran too. Too late, they realised they had come into an area where a constantly erupting geyser was at work. Even as they ran it plumed a boiling spray high against the stars and the men, running as fast as they could go, screamed and shouted as boiling water rained down on their naked backs. They no longer thought about ivory or anything else. Safety was the only thing that counted —

But there was no safety. The central geyser was not the only one. Smaller ones jetted viciously around the steam-blinded, scalded men. They had no idea where they were going. As fast as they moved the water, bubbling, was settling on the rocky ground and swirling round their feet. They tumbled down in it, seared to the bone by the boiling tide.

In five minutes the geyser stopped like a tap being turned off. In different parts of the basin the men lay groaning and burned in the midst of the water as it receded through cracks in the earth. Big Joe, smarting with agony, peered around him and made an ineffectual effort to get to his feet. One or two of the other men stirred, but hardly were they on their feet before the geyser started again and the deluge resumed.

There was no way out of the death

trap. The mutinous crew had run into a scalding blind alley and there they would remain . . .

And not many miles away, off the coast, Captain Hart had called together members of his own crew, and those of the tramp steamer. They had gathered on the deck under the stars whilst Hart addressed them.

'Something, somewhere, is decidedly wrong,' he declared. 'The first consignment of ivory and gold should have been brought here long ago: instead we have no sign of anybody, and certainly not of Mrs. Perrivale. The second batch of men who went out had radio equipment with them and should have sent back information, but nothing has happened. The only conclusion I can come to is that they are either dead, or else prisoners. I require twenty volunteers to go and look for them. The volunteers will take a radio with them and report every thirty minutes. You agree with that, Captain Simmons?'

The skipper of the tramp steamer nodded in the gloom.

'Nothing else for it, Captain. If it'll help

any I'll head the search party myself.'

'Thanks,' Hart acknowledged gratefully. 'I shall feel much happier if you do that. I must stay here and keep watch over the ships with a skeleton crew. On this part of the coast, and considering the kind of treasure we're trying to remove, I'm prepared for anything . . . All right, then, twenty volunteers needed, please.'

The men began moving in the starlight then, one by one, began to offer themselves . . .

★   ★   ★

As Anjani landed in the dust of Akada's main street with Tocoto on top of him he brought up his hands swiftly and locked them in his brother's throat, forcing his head upwards with all his strength. Realising what was intended Tocoto slammed down a terrific punch which left a bleeding gash on Anjani's cheek. Dazed for the moment he relaxed his hold and instead found his own throat seized in steel fingers.

Around the struggling pair the men of

Monango watched impassively, betraying neither interest nor enthusiasm. As far as they were concerned — and particularly as far as Barmono was concerned — this struggle was purely a business matter. The loser would die anyway, and so would the winner. From this there was to be no escape, but at least there was something interesting in matching the two vaunted jungle lords against each other.

The only sounds were the gasps and grunts of the two men, the thud of fists on bone and flesh, or the occasional horrified little cries from Rita as she was compelled to watch the proceedings. Her legs were so weak she was hardly able to stand, and indeed would not have done so except for the grip two of the blacks had upon her arms. Now and again, as the struggle between the brothers progressed the hard eyes of Barmono moved to the girl as he considered ways and means to dispose of her when the moment came.

A tremendous uppercut sent Anjani tottering backwards, but at the last moment he saved himself, made a quick recovery, and landed a straight-left straight into Tocoto's throat as he charged forward. He gulped and choked as the stunning blow paralysed his Adam's apple. He gulped and choked even more when a right and a left crashed in quick succession into his stomach. Hardly able to breathe and his head bursting with stars he toppled to the dust. Anjani jumped on top of him, seized the hair to jerk back his brother's head, and then he battered blow after blow into Tocoto's unprotected face.

He squirmed and gasped under the onslaught, finally forcing himself sideways. With his right hand he grasped Anjani's left ankle, close by, and twisted it with all his strength. Anjani set his teeth against the sudden pain and wrench, but since he was compelled to turn with his ankle he was forced from his brother's back and stumbled on his face.

Almost instantly a stunning impact descended on the back of his neck, at the base of the skull. Another one nearly blasted the senses out of him. Just in time he jerked his head to avoid the third and twisted over onto his back. He jack-knifed his legs and slammed out his feet, catching Tocoto under the chin just as he lunged forward.

He jerked upright and staggered slightly, and by that time Anjani had whirled to his feet and charged. As he moved he jumped, swinging himself well to one side so that the baffled Tocoto completely missed his objective as he landed out with his left. The next thing he knew Anjani was on his back, bringing into play that spine and jaw arm-lock which was his favourite trick.

Tocoto was compelled to drop to his knees, one sinewy forearm clamped under his chin, one massive knee planted inexorably at the root of his spine. His hands clawed the air helplessly as his head was forced further and further backwards under the terrific strain and the knee seemed to be driving straight through his body.

He screamed and twirled and twisted, but he could not dislodge the persistent, killing strain. Anjani never relaxed for a moment, using a steady and relentless tension that must finally result in the breaking of the neck or the spinal column. Before he had reached the crucial point, however, Tocoto suddenly went limp and offered no more resistance. Possibly it was pain that had overcome him.

Anjani remained motionless for a moment, ready for some kind of trick, but none was attempted — then he found himself dragged away by the men of Monango. Tocoto relaxed limply on his face and remained still. But there were signs of him breathing slowly.

'The fight is not over,' Anjani snapped. 'Tocoto still lives. He fainted with the punishment I gave him . . . '

'Kill him,' Barmono ordered implacably, motioning his hand.

One of the natives picked up a spear from beside him and came forward. Anjani, though held tightly, had not yet finished speaking.

'The right to kill Tocoto is mine!' he declared fiercely. 'Let him recover, then I will finish him.'

'We do not wait,' Barmono retorted. 'Kill!'

'Anjani — *don't!*' Rita entreated. 'Tocoto may still be your enemy, but he's also your brother. You can't let him be killed and you can't kill him yourself. It isn't — civilized!'

'I belong to the jungle,' Anjani answered simply. 'But if anybody kills Tocoto, I will!'

On the last word he abruptly snatched his mighty arms free of the grip upon them. At the moment the native was slamming down the spear towards Tocoto's back he received Anjani's tremendous uppercut straight under the chin. He was lifted from the ground and fell back six feet, collapsing helplessly with a broken jaw.

Anjani made one move forward towards the spear impaling his brother but was snatched back and held relentlessly. Barmono took hold of the spear jutting from Tocoto's back and dragged it free. Then he stooped and turned Tocoto over on his face. Blood was trickling from below his ribs where the spear had passed clean through him. He lay inert. Barmono stooped, listened at the great chest for a moment, then stood up again.

'Tocoto, jungle lord, dead,' he pronounced. 'Anjani, the last jungle lord, and white woman who help him, also die soon. Take them to sacrificial stone.'

Since neither Anjani nor Rita were well acquainted with Akada's ramifications they had no idea where the sacrificial stone was situated. All they could do was submit to being pushed and jostled from the main street and then through the many long, dead terraces with which the lost city abounded. So finally they reached a broad, grass covered region from the midst of which projected eroded stone seats, colonnades, and parapets. It was, in fact, a time-ruined replica of the arena in Monango where Rita had faced the sabre-toothed tigers.

'You sacrifice, you and white woman,' Barmono said, as Anjani and the girl were dragged to a halt. 'You die under day-stone.'

Not understanding in the least they found themselves seized again and lifted onto the shoulders of the captors. They were carried perhaps a dozen yards until, in the starlight, there loomed up a flat stone lying beneath a natural rocky tip. On the end of it, poised with point upwards, a massive rock spur stood, naturally balanced.

Anjani and Rita were commencing to grasp what was intended but there was just nothing they could do about it. They were laid on the flat stone, face upwards, their arms spread wide and roped into position. The stone was long, so Rita's feet touched Anjani's head as they were both fastened down immovably. Above them was the great starry abyss of the sky with the towering spur looming over them in terrifying insecurity.

'One touch of the finger can bring the day-stone down upon you,' Barmono explained, his voice grimly satisfied. 'It is called the day-stone because if a wet raffia rope be fastened to its summit and drawn taut, the rope dries swiftly with the rising sun. As it dries it lengthens, and — pushed by rocks that we shall pile against the spur — the spur tilts off balance. It comes down — as it has on many sacrifices in the days when Akada was rich and powerful.'

Anjani could think of nothing to say. Rita was silent too, her heart thudding heavily, her limbs aching from weakness. The way she felt at the moment she did not particularly care if she did die. At least, tied down as she was she was resting — and that was all she wanted. Rest — rest — rest.

Anjani raised his head slightly and watched what happened when Barmono had finished speaking. He saw the natives busy at work collecting massive stones which had fallen from the broken columns; another returned from some unknown part of the city with a long length of raffia plaited rope, and, perched on the shoulders of one of his comrades, went to work to make a big noose round the top of the spur. Anjani watched breathlessly, fearing that at any moment the stone might be sent off balance and come crashing down — but that would have been too quick a finish for Barmono's liking, and no mistakes were made. The rope was secured, then carried back to a nearby stone colonnade and fastened around it. From their own water bottles the natives soaked the plaiting until it began to shrink and with a faint creaking the mighty spur tilted slightly backwards on its balanced base.

Thereafter, between the supporting colonnade and the spur itself the natives began to pile all the rock and stone they could find, creating a tremendous pressure against one side of the spur which, when the rope slackened upon drying — with the coming of the sun — would tilt more and more over the hapless two below until it finally lost the perpendicular and crashed down upon them.

Anjani closed his eyes for a moment as he thought of that ghastly moment, then he opened them again to watch the natives leaving their task and reassembling around the watchful Barmono.

'Terrible Highness Mea avenged,' he said briefly. 'You cause her to die: you die too.'

This was all he said. With a jerk of his head he turned about and his men followed after him. There were the sounds of their departure for a while, then they died into silence.

Tocoto, too, heard them go. He was not dead despite the spear thrust that had been driven through his body. It had passed clean through, but the deflection at the last moment, caused by Anjani's attack on the native wielding the weapon, had prevented the barb from passing through any vital organ. Tocoto was hurt, badly hurt, and bleeding freely internally and externally — but he was not *dead*, and to a man of his tremendous constitution that was sufficient guarantee of his eventual recovery. The fact that his heartbeats had not been distinguishable to Barmono — who knew nothing of the more refined art of taking pulse beats — had been occasioned by the fact that at that moment Tocoto had been nearly finished, his life nearly destroyed by the shock of the spear blow.

But now he stirred, weakly, with extreme difficulty as the last sound of the retreating men of Monango died away. With every movement sheer torture he dragged himself through the dust and finally clawed his way to the still open doorway of the dwelling from which Rita had emerged. Tocoto knew that since she had been living there, there would be camping facilities of which he could avail himself.

Breathing hard and close to fainting he got to his knees and groped his way into the darkness beyond. His eyes were accustomed to the night so that, with the help of the starlight through the glassless window, he could presently make out the details of the interior — the bed, the extinguished lamp, the rifle, and then the boxes and odds and ends inseparable to a camp. Finally he discovered some cloth and wrapped a length round his wounded body. What had happened to him inside he did not know, but occasionally blood came into his mouth and he spat it out in disgust. By the law of the animals, water was the only real cure, so he drank some — and felt a little better.

Breathing hard he relaxed again, wondering vaguely what had happened to Anjani and Rita — then a memory came drifting back to him. When he had been lying almost unconscious he had heard Barmono speaking as though from far away. Something about a sacrificial stone. He knew where that was for, on his earlier visit to the city when he had stolen the jewel he had explored the ruin thoroughly . . . The jewel? It would be where he had been forced to put it. There was nothing to prevent him taking it away again, if he had the strength to get it. But first he must see what had happened to Anjani and the white woman, if only to satisfy his own longing for complete mastery over his brother.

He started to move again, holding on to the wall of the room to help him along, and so gained the doorway. Once here, he had not as much support to rely upon — but the sheer interest of discovering the fate of his brother and the white woman kept him going. Whatever had happened to his inside, he was no longer finding blood in his mouth, though it was appearing through the rough bandage he had tied about himself.

He kept on going, crawling and reeling

through the narrower streets, stumbling across the open spaces, until at last he gained the area which he knew to be the sacrificial arena. At the far end of it he paused, peering through the dim light of the stars and rising moon until he could descry the two figures bound flat on the table-like stone.

In spite of his pain and weakness he grinned to himself and went on again, finally reaching Anjani's side. Anjani turned his head to look and his lips tightened. Rita, too, looked, and a vague hope stirred her.

'I lost, and have freedom,' Tocoto said at last breathing hard and resting against the stone. 'True, I am badly hurt — but no more so than the beasts of the jungle sometimes, You, my brother, are doomed — like the white woman . . . '

Tocoto looked up at the towering spur and it took him a little while to figure out the meaning of the taut rope and piled-up cairn. When, he did so his grin widened.

'Barmono very clever,' he commented.

'Tocoto!' Rita called huskily. 'Tocoto!'

He turned to her at the mention of his

name, pausing with his elbows resting on the stone. Rita raised her head a little to be sure he was there and then lay back again. It was all she could manage with her arms drawn out taut to either side of her and bound underneath the rock with triple thickness of vine.

'Tocoto — you understand what — what I say?' Rita spoke haltingly in his own tribal tongue, as well as she could with her uncertain knowledge of it.

'Tocoto understand,' he replied

'You and Anjani — brothers. Same parents. Big sin to kill each other. Worse sin than killing stranger. Understand?'

'Tocoto only know jungle law.'

'Tocoto — not — *really* jungle man. Son of civilised man, like Anjani. I too civilised woman — not wild. You have been great enemies. Both too strong to be destroyed. You must become friends — as brothers should.'

Tocoto was silent, looking at the girl. He could see her eyes fixed on him in desperate entreaty, her face white in the dim light. After a long pause he answered.

'Tocoto and brother enemies — always

enemies. Tocoto lord of the jungle. Anjani will die leaving Tocoto with jewel. Tocoto the only master . . . '

'Tocoto, you can't!' Rita insisted desperately.

'Tocoto need mate,' he added. 'White mate like you. Tocoto take you.'

'No!' Rita screamed. 'No — I'd rather die than — '

She did not have the chance to say any more for Tocoto went to work on the ropes, unfastening the knots slowly. He had not the strength to do more. Until at length Rita found she was able to sit up. Anjani struggled vainly to free himself, tautening his arms and straining to the limit, but the vines would not part.

'Rita, free me!' he called. 'Tocoto shall not have you!'

With an effort Rita got a grip on herself. She was dizzy from weakness and the fear of what had been going to overtake her at dawn — but she was free. And Tocoto was having a struggle to keep his senses. These were the two things that counted.

She struggled down from the stone and

stood up, Tocoto watching her intently as he half slumped against the rockery, breathing hard and holding his anguishing spear wound. Rita took her chance and made a dive for Anjani's side. But before she could even start to try and unfasten the vine knots her arm was seized and she was flung backwards fiercely. Hurt though he was his strength was still far too great for Rita to grapple with.

As she flattened helplessly in the dust and saw Tocoto almost too pain-wracked to move after her, Rita remembered something. In the building where she had formerly been there was a ready loaded rifle. She was on her feet even as she thought of it. In her anxiety to seize this last chance she forgot all about her exhaustion and shaking limbs. She started to run as rapidly as she could, Tocoto breathing hard as he laboured to follow. He knew he could not make it, that the girl was getting further and further away — so he looked about him hastily and picked up a chunk of rock.

He felt as though he had torn his body

in half as he flung the stone unerringly. The wrench at his wounds brought a half-scream from his lips and it blended with Rita's own scream as the flying rock struck her a glancing blow across the side of the head. Her ears singing and lights exploding before her she tripped and fell, not stunned but certainly badly dazed. By the time she had started to recover the breathless grim-faced Tocoto had caught up with her. Savagely he seized her arm and dragged her to her feet.

'You not escape,' he told her roughly. 'You come with Tocoto!'

Rita knew her last chance had gone. With that iron grip holding her there was nothing more she could do, so she was compelled to submit as Tocoto bundled her along, down the main street, and finally out into the desert beyond the city. Presumably the jungle was his destination.

He moved slowly and always with painful effort, but even so his strength was enough for Rita to know that she could not again break free. Then she noticed something else which made her forget her own immediate predicament for the moment. Far away in the east there were the first grey streaks of the coming day.

Then suddenly Tocoto came to a stop, muttering to himself. He swung round so he and Rita were facing the city from which they had come. For a moment Rita's hopes rose as she thought that Tocoto had had a change of heart, but his next words dispelled the thought.

'Tocoto forget jewel. We go for it. Jewel give Tocoto all power he need.'

Rita did not answer, nor did she try and tear free of the grip upon her. She was commencing to hope that so much energy being expended would so wear out the badly wounded jungle man that he would perhaps collapse, or fall asleep, and give her another chance. For her own part she did not feel so weak as hitherto. The night air was fresh, the circumstances dangerous, both of which were conducive to making her more alert. There would probably be a shattering reaction, but at the moment she felt reasonably strong.

Tocoto too, to her growing uneasiness,

seemed to be slowly recovering. He moved with far more energy than hitherto, nor was he breathing as heavily when the entrance to the treasure-vault was reached. Since the stone had not been replaced over the entrance way Tocoto had no trouble on this score. He advanced into the darkness of the tunnel, still hanging onto Rita's arm. Knowing exactly where he had put the jewel he had little fear of it eluding him.

Rita began to struggle again as the blackness closed in. This was her opportunity to make another break for liberty, so she squirmed and writhed to the limit of her strength, but always Tocoto was too powerful for her. Finally his fingers tightened like a steel band round her upper arm and his voice came out of the darkness.

'You not escape, white woman. Tocoto need you. Only white mate in all jungle. You too afraid. Tocoto not hurt you.'

The assurance was cold comfort to Rita as she was bundled along in the dark. She could tell by the echoes when the treasure-vault had been reached, and for

198

a while Tocoto felt around in the blackness. So did Rita, with her free hand, and entirely by chance she found herself fingering some of the brick-shaped gold bars that were piled amongst the ivory.

Very gently, as Tocoto still held on to her and searched with his other hand for the rock pedestal holding the jewel, Rita dislodged the gold brick and weighed it in her hand. It was very heavy, and the perfect weapon. Tocoto heard the sound of the dislodgement and his voice came suddenly in the blackness.

'You do something, white woman. I heard you. *What?*'

'Nothing,' Rita answered, then having her direction from the sound of him speaking she suddenly swung up her free arm with all her strength and slammed the gold ingot down with terrific force.

It found its mark. Unable to see it coming, and having no warning, Tocoto took the blow directly on the side of the head. He gasped with pain and Rita felt his grip relax. Immediately she bolted into the blackness, blundered round in the dark for a while looking for the tunnel opening, and then raced up it as hard as she could go. To the rear she could hear Tocoto shouting in fury. Evidently he had not been knocked out despite the impact.

Rita arrived at the end of the tunnel to find it was coming daylight. She made one frantic and useless effort to push the stone barrier into position and failing, broke into another run. To get her rifle in time: that was the main need, then to release Anjani before sun-up, due now very shortly.

She had put fifty yards between herself and the enraged Tocoto before he appeared out of the tunnel mouth. Catching a glimpse of him over her shoulder she redoubled her efforts, gained the city's main street, then hurried along it to the building she had been occupying. In a matter of thirty seconds more she had the rifle in her hands and swung back to the door, in readiness to deal with Tocoto if he tried — as he would — to stop her heading for the sacrificial stone.

She regained the doorway and looked cautiously outside, the rifle ready for instant use — but Tocoto was nowhere to be seen. Too late she remembered what had probably happened. She twisted round to look at the window and at the same moment Tocoto came hurtling across the room.

In one savage movement he wrenched the rifle from her, then aimed a blow that sent her spinning backwards to crash upon the bed. She remained where she had fallen, panting and tearful, Tocoto eyeing her narrowly.

'Perhaps I kill you instead,' he said slowly. 'You wildcat. Too savage for mate.'

He advanced slowly towards her and her eyes remained fixed upon him in horror — but only for a second or two. Realising he had probably meant what he had said she rolled off the bed on the opposite side and made a lightning dash for the window. Tocoto grasped her intentions and was there before her, so she doubled back, dodged under his outstretched arm, and hurtled for the doorway. She had whipped up the rifle and was trying to get it to her shoulder when Tocoto reached her. The jolt his hand gave her arm jerked the trigger and the explosion was deafening.

Amazed, Rita watched. She could hardly believe her good fortune. The rifle barrel had been pointed at Tocoto's chest and now there appeared on it a welling crimson where the bullet had torn into him. Coming on top of his existing injuries the strain was too much and he crumpled slowly and became still.

Rita stood looking down on him for a moment, then still holding the rifle she blundered away down the street towards the sacrificial ground as the first rays of the sun beamed forth from dispersing mist.

She reached Anjani to find him struggling savagely to tear away the vines still holding his cramped and aching limbs. Above, the sacrificial rock was poised against the misty cobalt blue of the sky.

'Rita!' Anjani gasped, as he saw her staggering towards him with the rifle pressed against her. 'But what about Tocoto? What did he — ?'

Anjani broke off. Rita's face had gone

deathly pale from the strain she had been inflicting upon herself so soon after her illness. Gulping, and trying uselessly to speak she dropped the rifle, reeled forward, made one ineffectual effort to untie the vine knots, and then collapsed.

'Rita!' Anjani shouted huskily. 'Rita! Wake up!'

She remained slumped and motionless. He twisted and pulled in desperation, then looked above him again. The sunlight was brilliant now, shining full upon that deadly spur and the rope holding it. Possibly it was his imagination, but he could have sworn that the rock was slowly and imperceptibly bending inwards towards him as the weight of stone pressed it forward against the slowly expanding, drying rope.

'Rita! Rita!' Anjani yelled with all his lung power, in the hope that it might stir the unconscious girl back to life, if only long enough to unfasten his bonds. But she did not stir.

From above came a faint, ominous creaking sound. And then another sound from a different direction. The babbling of tribal voices. Anjani twisted his head in new hope and beheld half a dozen natives speeding towards him from across the grassy distances of the sacrificial arena.

In a matter of seconds they had reached his side. In breathless relief he recognised the men of the Untani, his own tribe, the men who had set out to find him and Rita and who had now evidently returned.

'Quickly!' he told them. 'Get me free! That stone above is coming down — !'

Keen hunting knives slashed through the vines in a matter of seconds and he tried to move, but cramp stopped him. He felt completely dead. So he was seized by arms and legs and dragged off the stone table just as there was a sudden mighty crack from above. The rope parted and the boulder swung outwards and then downwards. With a crash that split the stone table in two it came thundering down, chippings and javelins flying in all directions and narrowly missing Anjani and the natives as they stumbled back-wards, clutching the flaccid Rita in their midst.

When the haze of dust had slowly dispersed Anjani turned and faced the startled natives around him. He was more shaken than he cared to admit. Stooping, he picked up Rita's limp body in his powerful arms.

'I don't have to tell you what was intended,' he said, in the Untani tongue. 'You came just in time.'

'We returned finding no sign of you or the white woman,' the headman answered. 'Hear your shouts from stone — 'Reeta' — 'Reeta' — so came to look. We save the white lord.'

'And I'll always remember it,' Anjani said quietly. 'Now let us see if we can help poor Rita back to consciousness. Bring thunder stick,' he added, nodding to the fallen rifle.

Turning, he led the way out of the grass-strewn arena and so eventually to the main street and the building that served as headquarters. Behind him the Untani men followed. When he stepped inside the room that was serving as a camp Anjani stared in surprise, looking about him.

The bed with its overhead net had been torn down. The various camp accoutrements had been upended and smashed open. There was blood on the floor in various directions —

Anjani laid Rita down on the bed as one of the natives smoothed out the blankets, then he concentrated on the sole task of reviving her. Water and wrist-chafing finally served its purpose and she opened her eyes slowly. For a moment or two she obviously had difficulty in remembering, then as she saw Anjani studying her, her eyes brightened a little.

'Anjani! You're — alive! But — the stone — I was going to free you.'

'You took on too much, littler one,' Anjani murmured, and explained briefly what had been happening. Rita relaxed again in relief and glanced about her on the ebon giants regarding her. Then a thought seemed to strike her.

'But where is Tocoto?'

'Tocoto?' Anjani looked surprised.

'I left him here, or rather outside the doorway. I accidentally shot him in the chest and he collapsed . . . He must have recovered and escaped.'

Anjani made a signal to the men around him.

'Tocoto has escaped. Find his trail.'

They nodded and began moving swiftly, looking about them with eyes fully trained to the job. Several of them went outside, following the trail of bloodspots. One of them remained and picked something up from the floor. Excitedly he came across to Anjani and revealed his find in his black palm.

'The jewel of Akada!' Rita exclaimed in surprise. 'He must have dropped it when he was struggling with me and probably he was in too much pain to notice what had happened.'

'This becomes our property,' Anjani said, and he pushed it in the small pocket he had slit in his leopard-skin loincloth. 'Without it, Tocoto has no power over natives; no power over anybody. He is just an outcast wanderer of the jungle.'

'And a badly-wounded one,' Rita added quietly. 'Let it go at that, Anjani, and come back home with me — after we have moved the treasure, of course.

Tocoto has nothing left now the jewel has gone.'

Anjani nodded slowly. 'Perhaps you are right. I no longer love the jungle: only you. Where you go, I go . . . '

He looked up as the headman of the Untani returned with his fellow warriors.

'No trail of Tocoto beyond street outside, Mighty One,' he said. 'Tocoto been clever. Has covered trail as he has gone, hiding blood and footprints. He may be long way. He may be near. Not know.'

'Let it go at that,' Anjani responded. 'I no longer wish to follow Tocoto. I have proved in my battles with him that I am the master and he probably thinks I am now dead under the sacrificial stone. We will eat, rest and sleep — with you men guarding us — then we will start to remove the treasure as arranged to begin with.'

'Yes, Mighty One,' the headman agreed, grinning.

'You and the rest of you represent the Untani tribe — or what is left of it,' Anjani added. 'I promised the Untani should benefit from moving the treasure, and you shall. With Miambo, the Wise One, dead — you, headman, shall be in control and prosper from this and other trading.'

The headman's grin became all the wider.

'We will prepare meal,' Anjani said, 'Later, when we are rested, we will start our task.'

★   ★   ★

It was late in the afternoon before the party began its first moves to remove the treasure, prior to which Anjani gave the men full instructions. Rita, rested and fit enough to be on the move again, insisted on joining the party — so, in the evening sunlight, she, Anjani, and the assembled members of the Untani, every man of them, left the headquarters buildings and headed for the treasure-vault. It was exactly as Anjani had last seen it, with the massive guardian stone pushed on one side.

Torches were lighted and in a single

column, Anjani and Rita at the head, the men filed into the tunnel and at length into the treasure cave itself. For a moment or two Anjani stood considering the wealth that was presented.

'This will take two journeys,' he said finally. 'There is far more heavy ivory to be carried than can be done at one trip. You had better start sorting it out,' he added to the headman, 'then we can decide how to distribute the load. I will see what must he done with the gold.'

He turned to commence the task in the torchlight, Rita moving to help him, then he spoke up in sudden enquiry as there came a rumbling thud from somewhere up the tunnel. The busy natives looked around them too, baffled.

'That sounded like the entrance being shut!' Rita exclaimed after a moment. 'Tocoto pulled that trick on us once before, Anjani — do you think — '

Anjani hardly listened to her. He raced for the opening that led to the tunnel and then sped along the curving, gloomy vista. His worst fears were realized as, instead of beholding daylight ahead, there was only blackness. Finally he came up against the massive barrier stone. Behind him, Rita and the men of the Untani came hurrying and for a moment or two they stood listening to thuds and bumps from beyond.

'Tocoto!' Anjani yelled, with all his power. 'Tocoto, is it you?'

'This time you not escape, my brother,' Tocoto answered, his voice reaching faintly into the depths. 'I knew you would all go into the treasure vault, so I waited. Once before I trapped you here and you pushed stone away; this time you do not. I shall smoke you out — smother you, and nothing you do can save you. The stone is propped with more stones, and more stones again.'

On the outside of the stone Tocoto stood listening for an answer. He was blood-streaked and slow in movement but anything but dead. The bullet he had received from the rifle had only scored across his chest, and not entered his body. The spear wound, though damnably painful, was not sufficient to hold up his Herculean strength. He had worked patiently and cunningly for this moment, using a smaller rock to lever the giant stone and leaving it poised so it would fall into place at a mere push. Then he had concealed himself. Now he stood on a high mass of assembled rocks behind the stone and listened for the reply from those in the depths.

Anjani, however, did not trouble to reply. He turned to the grim faces in the torchlight.

'We can only try and push our way out, maybe prise away the rock with a tusk,' he said. 'Get two tusks,' he added to the headman. 'We'll see what can be done. The rest of you hold the torches nearer the barrier.'

His orders were obeyed and, on the outside, Tocoto set his mouth grimly. Finally he turned to the multitudes of low-growing bushes with which the slope down to the tunnel entrance was lined. He tore a quantity up by the roots and piled them close to the stone barrier. Inevitably, with the night wind blowing against the stone, the smoke would be carried into the tunnel through innumerable niches and cracks

— none of which, however, were large enough to permit of escape by those beyond.

Spinning a thin needle of rock between his palms Tocoto laboured patiently until he had a thin wisp of smoke amidst the tinder-dry vegetation. Finally, with his own blowing and the action of the wind the glow increased to flame and soon the underbrush was crackling fiercely.

Within the tunnel, as Anjani explored the massive stone and shoved uselessly against it, the smoke began to drift and set him coughing. He turned as two tusks were brought into view, their ends wedged into what small cracks could be found. Then there began a levering, shoving movement, Anjani and three natives operating one tusk, and four natives operating another. But, tough though the ivory was, there were limits to what it could stand. The delicately tapered natural points snapped under the strain and the rock remained exactly as before. Smoke was misting the torch flames now and setting everybody coughing violently. Since it had no outlet due to the wind blowing towards the tunnel entrance it began to become slowly denser.

Finally Rita could not stand the coughing any longer and went back into the main cave where the air was clearer. In a moment or two Anjani and the Untani men had followed her. They looked at each other in the torchlight.

'We're certainly not going to get out that way,' Anjani said, his jaw taut. 'We can't get enough breath to keep our strength up, and if the ivory breaks under pressure then we alone certainly cannot do anything.'

'But we'll be suffocated if we don't make some kind of effort!' Rita protested, rubbing her smoke-smarting eyes.

'Our only hope is that there is some way out of this cavern itself,' Anjani replied. 'We'd better start looking quickly — our best guide is the smoke. If it is drifting away anywhere then there is a gap that we can perhaps widen. Give me your shoulders,' he added to the headman, and then leapt upon them, finally standing up so that he reached the cavern roof.

The smoke was choking at this greater

height and, as much as he could, Anjani held his breath. In one hand he grasped a flickering torch and watched carefully which way the smoke was drifting. His final conclusions, as he came down to the cavern floor, were not reassuring.

'No trace of a gap whatever. The roof is completely solid and the smoke is collecting instead of drifting . . . We've got to make a final attempt to smash down that main barrier, if only to let the smoke out. If we don't we'll be suffocated within an hour.'

He jerked his head and the natives moved with him. Rita, unable to tolerate the incessant strain on her lungs, remained where she was, a lighted torch nearby. Holding their breath as much as possible Anjani and the Untani returned to the barrier and considered it.

'We push,' Anjani decided finally. 'Once before I escaped that way: with all of us trying we might succeed. Now . . . '

He put his mighty shoulder to the barrier, braced his feet on the floor, and then shoved with every vestige of his strength. To his own superhuman muscles were added those of all the men of the Untani who could find lodgement and their united power strained for several seconds to the uttermost limits.

Nothing happened. They relaxed coughing desperately and rubbing their eyes. The wedged stones outside were giving Tocoto the victory and the smoke was becoming intolerable.

'No use,' Anjani panted, tears streaming down his cheeks. 'Let's get back to the cavern . . . '

Rita did not need to ask how things had gone when she saw the expressions. Her own expression, between bouts of coughing, was one of growing terror.

'This means he's going to win,' she said at last, grasping Anjani's arm. 'If there's no way out — '

'There isn't, little one,' he told her quietly. 'Our united strength cannot move the barrier, ivory snaps against it, and there are no gaps anywhere that might give us a chance.'

'But — but we can't lie down and die, Anjani! We can't!'

Anjani shrugged. 'It is the law of the

216

jungle that if you have no way out, you die. Tocoto has won this battle and we cannot beat him.'

Rita said nothing. She was too stunned with the realisation that this was the end of the road, that death would come soon — coughing, coughing, smothering in ever deepening smoke, dying amidst incalculable wealth.

'Mighty One . . . ' The headman came forward, wheezing, and stood before Anjani.

'Yes? What?' Anjani glanced up at him.

'Smoke — not getting thicker. Maybe fire out.'

Anjani looked about him in wonder, then with relief. The black giant was right. The smoke was thick, certainly, but it was not increasing. Yet it was inconceivable that Tocoto could have run short of fuel since there were thousands of dry bushes near the tunnel entrance.

'Perhaps he's had a change of heart,' Rita said, her eyes hopeful. 'After all, he is your brother.'

Anjani smiled bitterly. 'My brother, little one, left me to die under the sacrificial stone. If he would do that he would smother me just as easily — '

A distant thudding and rumbling-interrupted him. It was coming from the tunnel entrance. Immediately Anjani, Rita, and the natives looked quickly in the direction of the smoke-ridden vista.

'Either more stones being added or Tocoto letting us out,' Anjani said. 'We'd better look.'

He turned swiftly and, followed by the others, hurried up the tunnel. The noises were still coming from outside and grew louder as the barrier was reached.

'Tocoto! Tocoto, what are you doing?' Anjani yelled. 'Are you afraid of the wrath of the gods at destroying so many living beings at once?'

'This is Captain Simmons,' a bass voice shouted back. 'Who's in there? Is it Anjani?'

'Captain Simmons!' Rita cried, nearly dancing with sudden relief. 'He's the tramp steamer skipper — *Can you hear me, Captain Simmons?*' she shouted.

'Mrs. Perrivale!' came a cry. 'Thank heaven we found you! Who's there with you? The rest of the crew?'

'No — only Anjani and the men of the Untani. Quickly, get us out — we're half choked with smoke.'

'Won't be long . . . ' And the noises and banging resumed as the rocks were shifted away. Then at last there came the glorious moment when fresh air came sweeping in as the main rock barrier was pulled away. Outside the heads and shoulders of the rescuers loomed against the stars. In the interval the night had come.

For a moment or two Rita was entirely taken up with explanations.

'We saw fire as we approached Akada,' Simmons explained, 'so, of course, we hurried to it and found these bushes blazing.'

'And Tocoto?' Anjani demanded. 'You did not see him?'

'Not a sign. He must have seen us coming and made himself scarce.'

There was a grim silence for a moment.

'All the rest of the boys are dead, then?' Simmons asked gravely. 'That's bad hearing.'

'I don't know whether they are dead or

not,' Rita replied. 'I know Mr. Crespin started off with Big Joe and some of the others, carrying ivory, but what's happened to them I can't say. You didn't pass them on the way and they didn't ever arrive at the ship?'

Simmons shook his head in the torchlight.

'I can imagine,' Anjani said grimly. 'There seemed to be a good deal of trouble among the men as it was: probably they tried to take the ivory for themselves. Either they will net a fortune and disappear for the rest of their lives — or else they fell prey to one or other of the jungle and desert dangers. In any case, forget them. We are safe, and so is Rita. That only leaves Tocoto, and my promise to myself unfulfilled.'

'He'll be in the jungle somewhere — or the desert,' Rita said. 'Let him stay there. There isn't a thing more he can do to us.'

'No . . . Not to us.' Anjani became silent, speculating on various possibilities. Then he glanced down as Rita took his arm again.

'Please, Anjani, for my sake — forget

220

Tocoto. Come back to England with me as you promised.'

He smiled. 'To clothes and burned foods and so called laws and regulations? You don't know what you are asking, Rita. I may tire of it very quickly, and come back here where one can be free.'

'Free!' Captain Simmons echoed. 'Great heavens, Anjani, you don't call it freedom to sleep in the trees and spend your days dodging wild animals, do you? The trip to here from the coast has nearly killed us and we haven't even touched the jungle yet.'

'We're of different worlds,' Anjani said, 'but just the same, Rita, where you go, I go. Perhaps I can learn to like civilised ways . . . The only cloud on my horizon is that my brother is still alive.'

'But he has no power,' Rita pointed out quickly. 'We have the Akada jewel, and that was the only thing that gave him any authority. On the other hand the survivors of the tribes he wiped out will be after him. There will be enemies everywhere, waiting to strike him down. I don't think you need to worry. Though it hasn't been actually left to you to finish him he will be finished just the same.'

'I have an obligation to the Untani, leaving them with Tocoto still free after all I promised,' Anjani said. 'I'd better hear what the headman thinks.'

He turned to him and explained the situation. The headman considered for a while and then gave his friendly grin in the starlight.

'Mighty One go where he chooses,' he replied. 'We of the Untani will start tribe anew. Some women of our tribe still live in jungle: we came upon them while we looked for you and the white woman. We shall mate again. Untani grow mighty tribe again.'

'And long before that happens I shall return and see you,' Anjani promised. 'Much trade between us. Akada only one city where treasure lie: three others too, according to Mea of Monango.'

At the mention of Mea, Rita glanced up. She had not understood the conversation itself, but the reference to the sinister high chieftainess stirred a memory.

'Anjani, this isn't the only city with

222

treasure to offer,' she said.

'So I just told the headman. We shall return, little one, when we have emptied Akada. Maybe we'll return for a long expedition to find the other cities of Beltanzi and Viljo. I shall be happy if I can always have the thought that one day I shall come back here.'

There was a silence. Then Captain Simmons cleared his throat.

'Well, that seems to cover everything for the moment, Mrs. Perrivale. I take it Mr. Anjani — if I can call him such — is returning home with us?'

Rita nodded and smiled in the gloom. 'He'll do more than that, Captain. He'll make me Mrs. — er — '

'Marry you?' Anjani asked. 'Of course! That is the only thing in life I want, and I cannot understand why there should be so many laws before I can do it. But you cannot become Mrs. Anjani. I had better take the name that you said you believed belonged to me. What was it now?'

'Hardnell. I believe you are the son of Mark and Ruth Hardnell of Zanzibar — just as Tocoto is a Hardnell too.'

'Tocoto remains Tocoto,' Anjani snapped. 'A jungle outcast — hunted, unwanted. A man-killer. One day, perhaps — ' He clenched his huge fists and then relaxed again. 'Sorry, Rita,' he said simply. 'I had forgotten. I am leaving Tocoto to the mercy of those he has ravaged. From now on I shall be Hardnell, not Anjani.'

'*Mr.* Hardnell,' Rita corrected, laughing. 'Later, maybe, we'll find your Christian name . . . '

'For the moment,' Anjani said, turning back to Captain Simmons, 'our job is to get this treasure moved out. I think we had better make a start, Captain — or at least when you and your men have had a rest.'

'We had one, just before we got here. Our only anxiety is to get the stuff moved and leave this dead city as far behind us as possible. It does something to your nerves.'

Anjani nodded and motioned towards the tunnel mouth leading into the treasure-vault. There was a general move as whites and blacks followed him . . .

THE END

*Books by John Russell Fearn
in the Linford Mystery Library:*

THE TATTOO MURDERS
VISION SINISTER
THE SILVERED CAGE
WITHIN THAT ROOM!
REFLECTED GLORY
THE CRIMSON RAMBLER
SHATTERING GLASS
THE MAN WHO WAS NOT
ROBBERY WITHOUT VIOLENCE
DEADLINE
ACCOUNT SETTLED
STRANGER IN OUR MIDST
WHAT HAPPENED TO HAMMOND?
THE GLOWING MAN
FRAMED IN GUILT
FLASHPOINT
THE MASTER MUST DIE
DEATH IN SILHOUETTE
THE LONELY ASTRONOMER
THY ARM ALONE
MAN IN DUPLICATE
THE RATTENBURY MYSTERY
CLIMATE INCORPORATED
THE FIVE MATCHBOXES
EXCEPT FOR ONE THING

BLACK MARIA, M.A.
ONE STEP TOO FAR
THE THIRTY-FIRST OF JUNE
THE FROZEN LIMIT
ONE REMAINED SEATED
THE MURDERED SCHOOLGIRL
SECRET OF THE RING
OTHER EYES WATCHING
I SPY . . .
FOOL'S PARADISE
DON'T TOUCH ME
THE FOURTH DOOR
THE SPIKED BOY
THE SLITHERERS
MAN OF TWO WORLDS
THE ATLANTIC TUNNEL
THE EMPTY COFFINS
LIQUID DEATH
PATTERN OF MURDER
NEBULA
THE LIE DESTROYER
PRISONER OF TIME
MIRACLE MAN
THE MULTO-MAN
THE RED INSECTS
THE GOLD OF AKADA